A Baby's Right to Choose

a novel

David L. Winters

"Then He will answer them, saying, 'Assuredly, I say to you, inasmuch as you did not do it to one of the least of these, you did not do it to Me.' And these will go away into everlasting punishment, but the righteous into eternal life."

Matthew 25:45–46

1

Madison pulled her five-year-old Toyota suv into the small parking lot. The non-descript, glass-and-steel building looked even less inviting than usual. A handful of protestors lined the sidewalk to greet her. As she turned off her car, several of the men shouted slogans like "Don't kill your baby" or "Give life a chance." Don't they recognize me by now? she mused.

Ignoring their taunts, her confidence rested in the large metal fence topped with barbed wire. She felt thankful and somehow comforted by the foreboding barrier as it kept the angry mob at bay. Although Madison had worked at the Springfield Women's Health Center for ten months, she never quite got accustomed to the anti-abortion zealots and their disgusting signs. Though not an everyday occurrence, the protests erupted like clockwork on Mondays and Saturdays. Happy Monday, thanks for coming by to scream at us.

Behind the smoke-colored glass outer door, Madison looked down at her bracelet and her new silver charm. Just the night before, her husband Zane had surprised her with the little tomahawk, symbolizing their trip to Wisconsin Dells. It had felt so good to get away for an end-of-summer vacation with the kids. Zane bought the charm as an anniversary gift at one of many gift shops that lined the quaint towns. Thinking about Zane, her mood improved as she entered the four-digit code for the inner door which led into the clinic's space, separating it from the other offices. Madison slipped her car keys into her Kate Spade purse as she waved to Vanessa behind the reception desk.

"You punch fast with that pass code," Vanessa said, smiling. "I didn't even get a chance to buzz you in. Hey, cute outfit. Where did you find pink slacks that went with that print blouse?"

"Macy's on sale," Madison replied. "Believe me, I had to look around for the pants. Good morning, by the way. How did your weekend go?"

Madison appreciated having a coworker like Vanessa. In a smaller office, it would be mighty lonely without the funny, outspoken redhead who loved all things eye makeup.

"Fine. Uneventful here on Saturday. I think the protestors spent their morning at the Knights of Columbus pancake breakfast. My son's basketball team won their game in the afternoon. Jarrett is so cute in his little basketball outfit. His team may go undefeated this year. How's Zane's wrestling squad doing?"

"The boys are about .500 so far. When you lose half your matches, no one is super happy. Zane calls it a rebuilding year; only a couple of seniors back from last year. Oh, before I forget, did you see the story in the paper about the woman killed in Snyder Park?"

Vanessa scrunched her nose. My husband hogs the paper. He mentioned the story, but I can't wait to hear the juicy details. Who manages to get themselves murdered in our little city? The whole thing would be exciting, except that I like taking the kids to that park. They have disc golf there. Nothing puts a damper on throwing around a Frisbee like an assailant stalking people from the bushes."

"I know, right?" Madison leaned on the counter to get closer to Vanessa. "I do worry about the way your mind works. You seem a little too giddy. Should I call the cops?"

"Stop it, silly," Vanessa said. "Of course, it's a tragedy and all. I'm just bored. What else do you know about the murder?"

"A jogger found the body. The dead woman was about our age. The killer clobbered the victim while she was out for a run. The police detective didn't say much in the newspaper interview - never do. They found the dead woman fully clothed—no sign of sexual assault."

"So creepy," Vanessa said. "Out for a jog and someone offs you."

"I know." Madison licked her lips and wondered if her lipstick needed a refresh. "Thank goodness that I've never been that fond of jogging."

The inner office door opened, and Madge Abzug stood staring at both women. Dressed in her usual pants suit and frilly scarf, she exuded business casual, except for her hair. Dyed a peculiar color somewhere between burgundy and magenta, her hair looked like it should have its own YouTube channel. Madison knew what Madge's glare meant. Madison shot Vanessa a low-key smile and walked toward the open door.

"Good morning, Ms. Abzug."

"Good morning, Madison," Madge said in her raspy baritone. "I need to speak with you before your first appointment. Set your stuff down and come to my office, please."

"Yes, ma'am."

Madison stopped by her own small office and shed her jacket. She tossed her purse in a desk drawer, nudging it shut with her shoe. Then she grabbed a pen and notebook before hurrying to the much larger corner office. Madge Abzug used a glass table for her desk. Brewer chairs made of wicker and metal alloy sat on the visitor's side of the table. Madison tried to make herself comfortable sitting in one of the chairs and stared at Abzug's weather-worn face.

"This will only take a few moments, dear. You've been around for almost a year now. There are a couple of matters we need to go over. First, we must do something about the cancellations. We've had at least one woman back out each of the last three Saturdays. This is just unacceptable."

Madison shifted uneasily in her seat. She'd seldom seen Madge angry, but her tone felt less than cordial. "I understand it's a problem, but I'm not sure what I can do about it. Some of these women are quite young."

"We need to come up with something," Madge continued. "Our doctor could get fed up and leave us. He doesn't get paid a ton for these procedures. I am going to be so angry if we lose him and have to look around for someone else. It's not that easy to find doctors who are willing to perform abortions and also have rights at an area hospital."

"I understand," Madison said.

"Look, you are doing a good job so far, kid. Obviously,

your heart is attuned to women and their reproductive health issues. However, it's time for *the talk*. Everyone gets a version of this discussion, so don't take offense. While I know some of your cases could have gone either way, your overall statistics indicate a reticence to recommend abortion. Is there anything I should know?"

Madison felt her face flush red. "Um, I'm not following you exactly."

"We want to stand with our clients. They have difficult choices to make, but obviously the right answer most of the time is abortion. Women ready for children don't visit a reproductive health center for evaluation. Something inside is telling them they aren't ready for a baby. Since they already know what's best for their situation, it's important we don't get in their way. Are explaining clearly the abortion choice?"

"Well, I guess so. Um, definitely. I'm with them whatever they choose." Madison shifted uncomfortably in her chair and loosened the top button of her blouse. Suddenly, her breathing felt labored.

Madge's eyes glared from behind her over-sized, black-rimmed glasses. "You don't have any confusion about morality or religious nonsense or anything, do you?"

"Oh no, Ms. Abzug. A woman's body is her own dominion. God gave us brains to make these difficult decisions." She knew this is the answer Abzug wanted to hear, but her own mother's disapproving face rattled around in the back of Madison's mind.

"Okay. Good answer. You have an appointment in just a few minutes. The client is only seventeen years old. Obviously, she probably needs an abortion. Let's make sure you help her get to the right decision."

"Understood," Madison said. Tucking away her pad and pen, she hoped this awkward meeting was ending.

"Okay. We will talk more later. Go, get prepared. Give her brochure 101-10. That has all the information she needs."

Madison stood up to leave, wanting to say more. No words formed in her mouth. "Thank you, Ms. Abzug. I'll go get ready."

She hoped that her long strides down the hall projected confidence, but inside Madison felt weak as a kitten. She wished she could think faster on her feet. Conversations with Madge Abzug were usually one-sided. Why can't I stand up for myself? Of course, I always explain the abortion option. That's why the clinic exists. We give women a choice about their future, but we're not running an abortion mill. Are we? We are here to do what's right for women and their bodies. Sometimes abortion is the right answer; other times it isn't.

The cramped office provided Madison little comfort. For some reason, she never brought a lot of personal things into her space. The gray, metal desk, a wooden coat tree and one tired filing cabinet did little to brighten her workspace. Several piles of pamphlets lay on the library table along the back wall. A picture of Zane adorned her desk, one of the reasons she went to work each day.

At Madge's suggestion, Madison kept pictures of her two children inside the desk. Clients didn't need to see pictures of happy, healthy kids when they were contemplating ending the little life growing inside them. Madge didn't say it that way exactly, but her convoluted explanation implied as much. In light of the talk they'd just had, the rebellious side of Madison wanted to take out the picture of her children and place it facing toward her next client. Just as she dismissed that idea, she could hear the outer door open. Minutes later, Vanessa introduced a trembling, young woman.

"You have a visitor. This is Ashley."

Madison got up from behind her desk and walked around to warmly shake hands with the young, blonde girl. As she greeted Ashley, Vanessa slipped behind Madison and placed the folder on the desk. Madison could see the inconspicuous pink tab sticking out of the folder. This indicated the client's urine test at the clinic confirmed the pregnancy. Vanessa gracefully backed out of the office, closing the door behind her.

"Hi, I'm Madison." She hoped her bright tone might ease the young woman's nerves.

"I'm Ashley," the young woman responded shyly.

"Ashley, thank you for coming in. Please have a seat there." Madison pointed to one of the two straight-back visitor chairs in front of her desk. Instead of returning to her usual seat, Madison sat down on the same side of the desk with Ashley. Less adversarial, this symbolically implied Madison's desire to be on her client's side. Madge had trained Madison that this projected caring. She would be there to support her client through the decision-making process. Both women angled their chairs to see each other better.

Ashley looked soul-crushed and quite nervous. Her straight hair surrounded an almost-angelic, if downcast, face. Light, creamy skin played against stunning blue eyes. Her feather-light hair flowed gently around symmetrical features and simple, gold earrings.

"I came just to get information." Ashley spoke in a guarded tone. Her beautiful face looked toward the door with determination, implying she might bolt out of the office at any moment.

"That's why we're here." Madison used her most reassuring voice. "We have all the information you need to make an intelligent decision. But first, let's talk more generally about you and your situation." Madison picked up the intake file Ashley had completed moments before in the reception area. "Let's see. It says here you are not currently married. You reside with your parents. Is that right?"

"Um. Yes. Is that a problem?"

"Oh honey, that's just fine. No one is going to judge you around here. We just want to understand your circumstances so that we can give you the best advice. It says you like cheerleading and listening to hip hop music. You are taking no medications and have no chronic illnesses. Is there a boyfriend in the picture?"

"Yes. My fiancée. His name is Terrell. He hasn't officially popped the question, but it's kind of understood between us. Oh, was I supposed to tell you his name?"

"It doesn't matter. Everything we talk about today is completely confidential."

With that, gentle tears began flowing down Ashley's cheeks. Madison reached for a box of tissues. Minutes passed as Madison let Ashley cry herself out. This is where the mourning process begins. *First, she must adjust to the situation she's in and then, the loss of the pregnancy.*

Finally, Ashley made eye contact. "I guess you are right. There really is no other way out. We don't have jobs or anything. What will my parents think? What if people at church find out?"

"It's your body and your decision. You know what's right for you at this time in your life. There is no reason a bunch of people need to know if you opt for a procedure. It's your choice. There's no reason to be embarrassed in any way. Smart women all over the world are taking control of their reproductive health."

Hearing herself, Madison thought she sounded like a women's lib matron of the 1960s—or what she imagined one to sound like. The words flowed effortlessly after almost a year at the clinic. Madison felt quite professional in her business attire spouting truisms about abortion. *Not bad for a 24-year-old.*

"I guess so." Ashley rubbed her eyes and flipped her hair back out of her face. "Can you tell me what happens if I do have, you know, the operation."

"The *procedure* is painless and only takes about an hour, including prep time. It's completely safe. The medical staff will take great care of you. We use gentle sedation. You won't feel a thing. We keep you for about an hour afterward to make sure you are fully recovered from the anesthesia."

"What do you do with, you know…what's left?"

"No reason to feel guilty. It's just some tissue that will be removed. It can't feel or know anything about what's going on. We dispose of medical waste according to state and federal guidelines. You may want to bring Terrell or another friend, if you like. It's not absolutely required. Some people like to have a friendly face in the waiting room afterwards … someone to drive you home." Madison could feel her face freeze in a hopeful, reassuring pose she'd practiced in front of the mirror. *Madge is going to love it when this woman commits to an abortion for this Saturday.*

Ashley's countenance changed from sorrow and regret to dogged determination. "How soon can you do it … the procedure, I mean?"

"Our state requires a mandatory three-day waiting period. The next time we have an opening is Saturday morning. So, the earliest would be this Saturday." Madison didn't mention that the small clinic only does abortions on Saturdays.

"Maybe I should wait until sometime the following week," Ashley said.

"You could, but usually in these situations, it's better

to go ahead and get the procedure scheduled and done. Then you can move on with your life. No sense in putting off the inevitable. For your own mental well-being, we recommend a complete break right at the beginning."

"Perhaps you're right. I don't know. Do my parents have to be informed?"

"No. Strictly speaking, in our state, they don't need to know, but there is the element of cost. Do you have insurance through your parents?" Madison hated to ask this question because younger clients sometimes delay things over financial issues.

"My parents have Blue Cross."

"That's excellent. If you use their insurance, your cost will be minimal. Chances are good they will learn of the procedure when they get a statement from Blue Cross. On the other hand, we don't have to tell your parents. Do you have enough funds from any other source? Savings? Credit card? You could sell something. Or perhaps the young man's family could help in some way?" Madison didn't mention that the parents of most teen boys would gladly pay for an abortion. It beats the alternative of saddling their son with eighteen years of child support before he's even out of high school.

"I'll have to ask him," Ashley started to sob again. "How will I tell him about this? What if he wants me to keep the baby?"

"Hold on a minute," Madison said. "This isn't his decision. It's ultimately your body and your choice. You may ask his opinion, if you want to, but don't give anyone else control over your life. Let me get you a pamphlet or two. The first booklet is about how to have difficult conversations with your man or your parents—if you *choose* to tell them." Madison reached behind herself to a table along the wall. Several pamphlets lined the credenza. "Let's see, um…birth control…cancer screening." She quickly selected one. "This is it, *Difficult Conversations*." She also picked up the one Abzug suggested: *Your Body/Your Choice*.

After more questions and several more minutes, Ashley looked relieved.

"Go home and rest," Madison said, handing her a business card. "This is my direct phone number. Call anytime, day or night. I'm glad to answer any questions you have. We can schedule your procedure with just a phone call."

"Thank you so much. You have really helped me think about things. I will probably have the procedure, but I need a little time to talk it over with Terrell."

"Let me show you out," Madison said, rising from her chair. "Take care, Ashley."

With that, the young girl walked away.

2

Detective Ernest Lawson stood over the body in the medical examiner's autopsy room. It wasn't the worst corpse he'd seen in fifteen years on the force. The body of the young woman showed little damage except for the obvious markings around her neck. Scratching his scalp, the veteran detective wondered what kind of criminal he was up against this time. Impatient by nature, Lawson disliked having to wait for a preliminary autopsy report. A quick trip to the morgue allowed him to gather information faster and, hopefully, develop some empathy for the victim. Connection to those involved in serious crimes motivated him and kept him going when others might slack off.

Medical Examiner (ME) Boris Rudner got up from his desk. Although he was in his 30s, Rudner appeared to

Lawson like he might be on death's doorway. Due to his gaunt appearance, pasty skin, and dark features, Rudner fit right in among the dead. The ME's jarring cough gave Lawson pause for his own health.

"Asphyxiation is the cause of death," Rudner said in a shrill, high-pitched voice. "The victim lost a minimal amount of blood. You can see a sharp line around the front and sides of the neck. Obviously, the perpetrator used a wire to strangle her. A rope or string would have left more abrasions and fuzzier markings. On the back of her neck, I noted numerous scratches consistent with the use of a garotte."

"Garotte." Lawson repeated the word before sighing pensively.

"It's a specific kind of device for killing. You string wire, usually piano wire, between two pieces of wood. Tie knots in the ends. It allows you to handle and twist sharp wire around a victim's neck without leaving wounds on the hands of the killer."

"Yes, I know what a garotte is…" Lawson's voice belied irritation.

"This weapon is kind of specific. I can tell you that no crimes with a similar killing device have been reported in twenty years around this area. I get bulletins from the State Medical Examiner's office too. Nothing like it has been reported as the murder weapon in that publication either."

Lawson asked, "What else can you tell me about the victim or the body?"

"She wasn't sexually molested or harmed in any other obvious way," Rudner said. "The body contains no bruising or abrasions. I took samples from under her fingernails, but I don't expect there to be any foreign DNA. She probably didn't have a chance to put up a fight. Somehow, the killer took her completely by surprise."

"No marks on her knees or legs," Lawson noted. "Can you be pretty sure the attacker didn't knock her down or trip her?"

"The shins and legs show no signs of trauma. Her jogging suit is bagged over there, but I went over it with a fine-tooth comb. It certainly appears that she stopped on her own to talk to whoever killed her. Otherwise, there would have been some sign of struggle. Perhaps she recognized her killer, certainly didn't feel threatened. If I learn anything else significant, you will be my first call. Otherwise, the preliminary report should be out by the first of next week. It has to go through the signature chain here."

"Thanks, doc. I hope to hear from you soon. Right now, we don't have much to go on."

3

A loud whistle pierced the mayhem unfolding in the auxiliary gym. "Okay, that's it for today," Coach Zane Matthews yelled. "Stack up the mats and grab your gear. I don't want the equipment guys here all night picking up after you."

Terrell and the other high school boys quickly disassembled practice mats and hauled them to the storage area under the bleachers. As required by Coach Matthews, no one moved toward the locker room until the last mat slid into place.

"Pretty good practice, Coach," Athletic Director Nate Underwood remarked.

"They worked hard today," Coach Zane replied. "We still have a way to go, but they are a young team."

Terrell didn't particularly like Underwood. He gave long, boring speeches at pep rallies and during the awards banquet at the end of the season. As the two men continued talking, Terrell and the other wrestlers headed downstairs and began stripping out of their practice uniforms. The sound of the showers springing to life added urgency. Although he liked wrestling, Terrell hated showering twice a day. His mom had this policy about a shower in the morning before school. Coach required everyone to shower after practice. He called it de-funking before returning to polite society, whatever that meant. Although required, Terrell spent the minimum amount of time soaping up and rinsing off.

A few of the other guys soon joined Terrell, toweling off and getting back into their street clothes. Before long, a small crowd formed, waiting for the usual post-practice chatter. Although one of only two African-Americans on the wrestling team, Terrell was a natural team leader, partly because he won all of his wrestling matches and partly because of his outgoing personality.

Grinning, Scott said, "So, it looks like you were getting pretty friendly with a certain cheerleader Friday night."

"Yeah, you two were going at it hot and heavy after the football game," Rich agreed. "She must be a great kisser."

Terrell liked both guys, but hated when they started talking about his girlfriend. "She's a sweet girl," Terrell said. He knew they meant Ashley Featherstone, cheerleader, straight-A student, and his steady girlfriend. Although dating for several months, they had only recently begun showing affection in front of their classmates.

"Super sweet looking," Scott teased. "Word is she goes the whole nine yards to please her man."

Another boy standing nearby hooted and smiled broadly at Terrell.

"I'm not a brother that kisses and dishes," Terrell said, feeling anger well up. He tried to stay cool while buttoning his blue Tommy Bahama shirt, then tucking the shirttail into his pre-washed jeans. "We enjoy spending time together. That's all I am going to say."

"Since when?" Scott asked. "You gave us the blow-by-blow when you were dating Lashonda."

Scott can be so rude, Terrell thought. He decided it was best to get out of the situation before it escalated. "Let's just say Ashley's the best. She's the whole package, beautiful, smart and sweet. I don't want to mess up a promising relationship." Terrell zipped up his leather gym bag just as Coach Matthews entered through the heavy, metallic gray door.

"Terrell, nice pin in practice today."

"Thanks, Coach," Terrell replied. He felt his lips curling into a smile. The thing he coveted most, Coach's admiration, fueled his ambition. Every dream about wrestling included coach hugging him and handing him a trophy after the big win.

"That isn't all he's been pinning," Scott said to a few hoots and hollers from the other boys standing around. "Terrell's got a new lady."

"Scott, you need to put a lot more time into lifting weights and less time gabbing," Matthews said, shooting an intimidating look toward the chiseled wrestler standing a foot away.

Coach Matthews inspired awe in his wrestlers. A three-time state champion, he remained fit and fearsome. He stared at each wrestler's face for a hint of insubordination. They all stood quietly, knowing that any response would bring hell to pay in the next practice. Terrell used the opportunity to exit up the stairs and head out into the bright sunshine.

From a distance, Ashley looked like an angel. She leaned against her white Mustang, a gift from her parents at her Sweet 16 party. Her straight blonde hair moved a little in the breeze like feathers from angel wings. Terrell could feel an ear-to-ear smile creeping across his face. Her black-leather jacket, well-fitting black jeans, and soft pastel shirt sent his temperature rising. He wanted to hug her tightly and press his body next to hers, but something seemed wrong with her expression. She always smiled at him when he came into view, but not today. *What have I done now?*

"Hey Babe, what's going on?" Terrell tested the waters.

"Hey," Ashley responded with a peck on Terrell's cheek. "Jump in the car; let's talk on the way home."

Terrell knew before they pulled out of the parking spot that big trouble lay ahead. He tried to slip is arm around behind her head, but she gave him an irritated glance. What could it be? Did one of her girlfriends put some stupid idea in Ashley's head? Everyone seemed intent on messing up their relationship.

"Is everything okay?" he asked, hesitantly.

"I had an appointment at the clinic today." Her voice was flat.

"Oh. Is it anything serious? Are you alright?"

"I'm pregnant."

The words hit Terrell like a body slam into the wrestling mat. He couldn't think or fully process what she said. Suddenly, breathing came with difficulty. More than anything, he wanted to jump out of the car. He needed to run away right now. Maybe he could jog home, get in bed, and pull the covers up over his head. This situation could not be real. Would Ashley follow him, pursue him? Maybe her dad would come after him with a shotgun.

Trying to sound cool, he started to say something. He

meant to ask how she knew, but the only thing that came out was the word *how* about three octaves higher than he intended.

"Well, I think we both know how!"

Terrell felt defensive. "I know that," he said indignantly. Then, more softly, "Are you sure?"

"Sure what? Sure, I'm pregnant? Sure it's yours?" Ashley's voice revealed her growing anger.

"Hold on, baby. That isn't what I asked, and it isn't what I mean."

"What *do* you mean?"

"I just want to understand what's going on," Terrell said. "Obviously, this is a big deal."

"You are darn right it is," Ashley responded.

Terrell thought for a minute, knowing anything he might say could and would be used against him, perhaps in a court of law. Babies are a major thing. Suddenly, he didn't want to run away. He wanted to stay and talk to Ashley, help her figure this out. He would stay close as long as she needed him.

"Let's get some French fries," Terrell said.

Ashley pointed the Mustang in the direction of Mabel's Kitchen, the greasy spoon diner where they met and fell in love. Over the past few months, they shared burgers and fries and gigantic milk shakes. It became their place for chow and holding hands, for falling in love. Once inside, they made their way to their favorite booth, both sitting on the same side of the table, just like always. *Perhaps, nothing has to change,* Terrell wondered.

"We'll take two soft drinks and one large order of fries," Terrell said. The sixty-something waitress seldom said much to him. Wanda nodded and quickly scribbled the request on her order pad. She knew Terrell and Ashley from numerous visits, but Terrell suspected she didn't particularly care for their romance. *Perhaps she's a racist ... Maybe she doesn't approve of the black man getting involved with a white woman.*

"Did you take a test or something?" Terrell asked.

"Of course, two of them," Ashley said. She began to cry, tears gently rolling down her cheeks. "And that was just at home. Then, I went to a clinic. All of the tests came back positive, I'm really pregnant."

"It's okay, baby. I can take care of you. We can keep the baby, start a family together. Home Depot is hiring."

The words rolled out of Terrell's mouth, but he wasn't sure where they came from. Did he really want to set up housekeeping with Ashley and a baby?

"You want to marry me?" Ashley turned toward him and dabbed her mascara with a paper napkin. Her voice softened as she thought about a big church wedding.

The question rocked Terrell. He hadn't thought far enough ahead to consider the marriage issue. After thinking a minute, he said, "In good time. We have to get through school, get jobs."

"I'm going to college," Ashley said resolutely. "How can I do that with a baby?"

"People do it all the time," Terrell said. "Just relax and don't make any rash moves. We are in this together. We are a thing: baby or no baby."

Some of Terrell's favorite college athletes posed with their children after football games. He knew that some college students had children. Practically speaking, he had no idea how that worked or even if the men lived with their children or in some sports dorm. He could ask Jason, one of his wrestling teammates. Jason's brother plays basketball for Purdue.

Ashley looked somewhat relieved as the French fries arrived. After pulling a bottle of ketchup from her apron,

Wanda left them without a word. Terrell nodded, and Ashley squirted ketchup liberally on the fries.

Terrell hated the way Ashley ate fries. Instead of putting the ketchup neatly to the side, she insisted on pouring it directly on the golden-brown potatoes. She then ate them with her fingers, resulting in messy, ketchup-y hands. Why couldn't she use a fork? Earlier in their relationship, he didn't mind so much. This day, it bothered him a lot. How could he spend his life with someone who grossed him out?

"Why don't you use a fork?" Terrell asked testily.

"What are you talking about?" Ashley asked. "This is how I always eat my fries."

"It's gross. Can't you just use a fork. Look at your fingers. They're a mess."

Ashley looked down at her fingers. She grabbed several napkins from the holder then furiously wiped her fingers in an exaggerated motion. She picked up her fork, then set it down and began to cry softly.

Wanda shot Terrell a dirty look from the lunch counter. Shaking her head, she wandered back into the kitchen to give them a little privacy.

"Let's just go," Ashley said. "I don't want to eat right now. My stomach hurts, and I'm getting a headache."

The idea of leaving sounded great to Terrell. Suddenly, his desire to run bubbled up again. He looked at the bill that Wanda left for them.

"Can you pick up the tab, baby?" Terrell asked sheepishly.

"Sure," Ashley said. "I can take care of it. I can take care of everything. You say you plan to take care of me and a baby, but you can't even afford an order of fries and a couple of cokes?"

"I will jog home from here," Terrell said. He stood up to leave.

"Terrell!" Ashley called after him, but he didn't turn around.

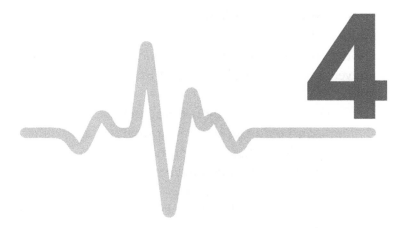

Madison loved her kitchen. The pale blue, shaker-style cabinets, white quartz counter-tops, and indigo subway-tile backsplash made her grin every time she walked into the room. Her Mom was right: the kitchen is the center of the home. On their own, she and Zane could never have afforded the extensive re-do of their aging Craftsman. A generous cash wedding gift from Zane's parents paved the way for many upgrades. Now the two-story gem reflected the best of the past and all the convenience of modern technology. The wine fridge, the Viking gas range, and huge side-by-side Sub-Zero refrigerator surrounded her whenever she cooked.

"Mommy, Braden is tearing up my coloring book," Shelby complained.

"Honey, you know that he doesn't understand yet. He's just a baby. Put your things away like I told you. If you put them away when you are done, he won't think to bother them."

Shelby scurried back across the open-concept great room and ripped her coloring book away from her little brother. Braden protested with a short squeal, but quickly moved on to the purple bear that Shelby set in front of him.

"That's your toy," Shelby said resolutely.

Madison heard the back door opening and Zane's footsteps as he walked through the mud room. Seconds later, two strong arms engulfed her from behind, his lips nuzzling her ear. She giggled as his five-o'clock stubble rubbed against her neck while pulling her close. She gazed into those clear, brown eyes while running her right hand up and down his back.

"Sweetie, I'm so glad you're home. Dinner is almost ready, and I'm starving."

"Everything smells fabulous," Zane said. "You even made a little salad for us. Nice."

"Go wash up. I just have to rescue the garlic bread from the oven and set the lasagna on the table."

Zane gave Madison a final squeeze and made a beeline for Shelby. Scooping up their daughter high into the air, he blew raspberries on her tummy as she descended to face-level. The little girl laughed uncontrollably until he set her down on the over-stuffed couch. Staring into her father's face, Shelby beamed pure affection. Madison loved Zane all the more as she watched him play with their four-year-old.

"How's the sweetest little angel in the world?" Zane asked, staring deep into her eyes and surveying her chubby cheeks.

"I'm wonderful, Daddy. Thanks for coming home to me."

"Let's go wash our hands so we can eat the delicious dinner your mommy prepared."

On his way to the half bath, he grabbed Braden and swung him over his shoulder. Patting him rhythmically on the diaper, Braden let out several gaga sounds matching the patting cadence. Then the trio disappeared down the hall.

Madison placed the salad on the table and began plating up the meals for her and Zane, as well as a smaller portion for Shelby. She used tongs to pull individual pieces of garlic bread out of the oven. Braden had eaten an hour earlier when Madison first arrived home from Grandma daycare.

While the three ate and laughed over the decadent lasagna, Braden happily danced up and down in his toddler swing nearby. His joyful sounds formed a sweet backdrop to the chewing and clanking going on around the table. Eventually, he tired himself out and collapsed into sleep.

"I don't know how you get it all done," Zane said, smiling toward Madison. "You worked at the clinic today, retrieved the kids, fed the little one, and made this fabulous meal."

"That's why they call me superwoman," Madison said playfully. "Actually, I assembled the lasagna yesterday and just popped it in the oven after work."

"Mommy, may I leave the table and go watch my princess show?"

"Sure, honey," Madison said, picking up Shelby's napkin. "Let me wipe your hands. I will join you after Daddy and I finish."

Shelby carefully climbed down from her booster seat and bounced into the family room. Madison pushed back from the table a few inches and looked at Zane. "Do you ever wonder why we are so blessed?"

"Every day," Zane said. "Coming home to this house and my dream girl is the best. The kids, my job as a wrestling coach—life is everything I've ever wanted." He reached over and held Madison's hand for a moment before returning to the lasagna.

"Today at the clinic, a young girl came in. She couldn't be much out of high school. My heart went out to her."

"Pregnant?"

"Yes. Scared to death. Didn't want to tell her parents. No money of her own."

"Did she make you feel guilty?"

"Here I am, perfect everything. I've got two beautiful children, a fabulous husband who's a good provider, and we live in my dream house."

"Yep. It's hard to say why some people seem to get all the breaks, and others run into so much trouble. You said she's young though."

"She's drop-dead gorgeous: blonde, cheerleader, dating a wrestler. Oh no." A horrified look swept over Madison's face. "Forget I said that. I shouldn't have told you. What if she goes to your high school? The wrestler could be one of your boys. I violated her privacy rights. I could be fired for that."

"Relax. I'm good with secrets. HIPAA or not, I promise not to rat you out to the Feds." Zane smiled and reached over to touch his wife's shoulder. "You never tell me about your clients. You seem rattled. Something must be different about this girl. Did she get to you?"

"I guess so. We see women at various stages of their reproductive years. The young ones always make me think. Really, that's why I work there. When I had my abortion all those years ago, no one helped me. I couldn't tell my parents. You know how my mom is – all religious and everything. There was no compassion before or after. No one took care of me when the procedure ended. They just sat me on a hard, wooden chair in the lobby and told me not to leave for an hour. I felt so empty, like all the life got sucked out of me."

"If I'd known you then, I would have gone with you."

"Yes, I know you would have. If I had known you then, we probably would have kept the baby. That's why we're together now. I made my mistakes and learned from them. I figured out how to recognize a keeper when I saw one." Madison moved from her seat and kissed Zane squarely on the mouth. She stroked his curly brown hair and then traced his strong jaw with her finger.

"Oh, I meant to ask you," Madison said. "Did you hear about the woman murdered on the jogging/bike trail?"

"Yep, one of the other coaches told me about it in the teacher's lounge. As he read the article, it sounded like she might have jogged along Mason Boulevard and then headed into the park from there. That's on the way home from the school. We had the church picnic near there last year, remember?"

Their conversation continued in the living room until time for Shelby to join Braden in sleepy time. Madison took a minute to comb her own hair while Zane put Shelby down. She heard him retelling the same bedtime story Shelby requested every night for the past three weeks.

What could that murdered woman jogger have been thinking? Madison asked herself. *No one gets killed in this sleepy town. Perhaps she felt totally safe. The television news said that the woman lost one pink running shoe as she tried to evade her killer.* Madison imagined the woman jogger's fluid steps, interrupted by something ... but what? Did creepy eyes track her as she ran? Did she die like a svelte gazelle, felled by a Serengeti predator?

The killer must have lured the young woman with some ruse, perhaps interrupting her lengthy strides that propelled her along the bike path. Maybe a madman got her to stop by asking directions or pretending he needed her phone. Madison fell deeper into morbid curiosity.

"The police found the body only twenty-five yards from Mason Boulevard, dragged off the running trail into a ravine," Madison said as Zane returned to their bedroom. "The newspaper said the killer strangled the woman to death. Although healthy and a little taller than the average woman, police theorized the attacker must have been taller still and quite strong."

Zane just looked at his wife with sleepy eyes. He took off his pants and socks at the side of the bed. The sight of his taught, hairy body sent shivers of excitement down her spine. Moments later, he snored loudly next to Madison.

Madison wondered what she might do. No way would she stop and talk to a young man on the running trail. If he appeared hurt, would she stoop down to help him? What if he wrapped a wire around her throat? Her hair bristled on the back of her neck as she imagined coming face to face with a killer. Although terrifying, she also found it quite exhilarating. How would it feel to have a vicious strangler working his way around behind her and dragging her from the safety of the bike path? What would it feel like to have the life slowly choked from her body by some maniacal killer? She'd definitely fight to see her children and husband again, but what if the attacker just proved too big, too strong?

5

Madison hated this part of visiting her OB/GYN doctor. Sitting in a gown, waiting for Dr. Heller to enter the examining room, she felt exposed and lonely. Even though her doctor was a kindly, older gentleman, he was still a man. No female gynecologists practiced in this smallish city. The only option to see a woman OB/GYN would be to drive thirty-five minutes to the next larger city up the highway. With all of her commitments, Madison didn't have time to be so choosy. Although her doctor visit would end up in joyous confirmation of her suspicions, the wait in the patient gown brought back horrible memories that she wished to forget. Moments before, the nurse practitioner drew the blood sample. Now, Madison just waited.

It seemed like several minutes, and she could occasionally hear voices from the adjoining examining room.

"Hey, Madison, how are you?" Dr. Heller smiled warmly as he entered the room.

"Oh, Dr. Heller, I'm fine." Madison couldn't help but smile at the massive figure in front of her. Although shrouded by a white lab coat, anyone could see Dr. Heller needed to lose at least a third of his body weight. Balding on top and gray on the sides, he looked every bit of his mid-sixties age.

"You are more than fine. You are indeed pregnant, young lady. Not too far along, but definitely pregnant."

"Those home tests are getting pretty accurate," Madison said smiling.

"Going to put us old docs out of business one day. Let's check you out and make sure you are healthy and up for another run through your paces."

As he began the physical exam, Dr. Heller became all business. No chitchat as he made a few guttural sounds with his throat that probably had more to do with phlegm, than anything he heard or saw. After taking her blood pressure and listening to her heart and breathing, the rest of the exam couldn't have lasted more than five minutes. Then, he pronounced Madison healthy and ready to gestate. After he left the room, Madison breathed a sigh of relief and quickly put her clothes back on.

As her sweater came down over her head, she caught a glimpse of her own face in the mirror. Still pretty by any standard, but she thought she saw the beginnings of a wrinkle near her left eye. She could find no gray hairs in her neatly-trimmed brown hair, though she searched for them often. Maybe she could enjoy having one more baby without totally undoing the figure she fought so hard to maintain by skipping lunch most days.

At the reception desk, Madison paid her $30 co-pay. "He wants to see me back in 60 days."

"Okay, can you come back on Friday, January eighth at 9 a.m.?" the scheduler asked.

"That's really not the best day for me. Can we make it a Saturday?" Madison asked. "I want to bankroll my sick leave for the time off following the birth."

"Oh, I'm sorry. He doesn't come into this office on Saturdays. How about lunchtime on the eighth?"

"That could work," Madison said. "Can we make it 12:30 p.m.?

"Yes. Let me write you out a card."

Madison left the office via the front door and made her way to her suv. She saw Dr. Heller clumsily climb into the driver's side of a black Mercedes. *He must have gone out a rear exit.* Madison still had things to do, so she quickly tossed her purse in the car and headed to the market.

6

The black luxury car turned into a circular driveway and continued around the other two cars parked closest to the stately, two-story, brick colonial. The doctor pulled into his usual place near the maple tree. Dr. Heller retrieved his satchel and suit coat from the backseat. Walking up the stairs to the front entrance, he paused between the large columns supporting the roof and two-story portico. As he stood there thinking, the door opened and his wife Marie greeted him.

"Welcome home, Jerry," Marie said, kissing her husband on the cheek, as was her custom.

He heard quick footsteps coming from another room, and soon Cynthia planted a kiss on his other cheek.

Noticing she'd left a little lipstick; she used her thumb to rub it off.

"Welcome home, Daddy. Short day today?"

"Cynthia came down from Chicago for a visit," Marie quickly interjected. Usually dressed more casually around the house, Marie sported a silk, cream-colored blouse and crisp, navy-blue, medium-length skirt.

"I see," Dr. Heller said. "Not a particularly short day, Cynthia. I started at 8 a.m. at the hospital and spent the early afternoon at my practice. I've told you on your last visit that I'm trying to cut back my hours. Someone my age should be retired by now."

"Oh Daddy, you love your work too much to ever retire." Cynthia said.

"Don't you, dear?" Marie asked.

"Suppose so," Dr. Heller replied. "Where were you two sitting? I'll join you in a moment."

"In the kitchen," Marie said. "Set your stuff down and come have some coffee with us. Cynthia's been watching me bake pies and regaling me with stories of big city life. We simply must get up to Chicago again soon. She found another interesting art gallery near Water Tower Place. I want to eat in fancy restaurants, shop for clothes, and go to the theater again."

"We go to shows here." Dr. Heller protested momentarily. "Oh, never mind. I will take you to Chicago in the spring."

He knew it made no sense to object. After all these years of marriage and with their bank account fatter than a squirrel's cheeks in November, they could spend a little money on fancy dinners and Chicago hotel rooms. What was the sense of making all that cash and not spending it? Although he worried about Marie's future after he was gone, he secretly loved being a big spender. He would strut up Michigan Avenue in a suit, buying Mrs. Heller clothes and watching her face light up from the attention.

Dr. Heller put down his satchel and jacket on the library table in the hall. After glancing through the mail, he followed Marie through the central hall and into the kitchen.

"So, tell me Cynthia, how are you?"

A fortyish woman with short, dark-brown hair and bright-red lipstick looked at her father through round, black glasses. "Daddy, it's so nice to be home—dreadful as your little Springfield remains."

"Give it a rest, Cynthia," Dr. Heller said. "*Little* Springfield paid for your Brandeis education, and I still pay half of your mortgage in Chicago. We must not be doing too badly out here in the hinterlands." Softening his tone, he continued, "I always forget the beauty of your green eyes."

"Touché, Daddy. Change the subject; that's the way to do it. Anyway, how are you? I hope you decide to retire soon. Take Momma on an endless cruise around the world. You two deserve some rest and relaxation. Momma told me that you still work fifty- to sixty-hour weeks. I don't see how you do it: pregnant women all week and abortions on the weekend. Do they still scream at you entering the parking lot over at the clinic on Saturdays?"

"Those religious nuts aren't going to keep me from doing what needs doing. They're harmless. Some of the most radical creeps have been coming to the clinic for twenty years. Too bad someone didn't abort them years ago."

"Jerry!" Marie exclaimed.

"I worry about someone hurting you," Cynthia said in a softer voice. "You hear about zealots shooting doctors every once in a while."

"Christians can be such a bunch of hypocrites" Dr. Heller said. "They supposedly despise murder of the unborn.

However, every now and then, one of them knocks off an abortion doctor. The wackos at our clinic don't represent sweetness and light with their chanting and waving disgusting signs."

"Very few people in town even realize your dad is the only doctor who does abortions in Springfield," Marie added.

"Unless a woman avails herself of my services, most have no idea. I'm going to retire when I'm good and ready. It may be sooner than you think. You better find a way to make more money with that art degree of yours or else find another husband that can keep up with your taste for life's finery."

"Interesting you should mention men, Daddy." Cynthia looked down at her coffee cup, swirling the remaining brown mixture around a time or two.

"Let's hear it," Dr. Heller said curtly.

"I have indeed met an interesting man; Jacob Fields is his name. He's not wealthy, but he works for Social Security Administration downtown in the Loop."

"Oh honey, that's great," Marie interjected excitedly. "What's he like?"

"Without sounding all starry-eyed, which I am, he is about the most amazing man I've ever met. Drop-dead gorgeous—in a very masculine way—doesn't do him justice. He has luscious dark hair and strong shoulders. When he holds me in his strong arms, whoa! His hands are gigantic. And he bought me this beautiful ring." Cynthia stuck out her hand to reveal a tastefully-sized diamond, oval-shaped and sparkling. Marie took her daughter's hand and studied the ring carefully before smilingly sweetly at Cynthia. "It's so nice."

"Where did you meet this new man of yours?" Dr. Heller asked.

Pausing, Cynthia pursed her lips and looked up from her coffee cup. "I met him at my Alcoholics Anonymous meeting."

The news surprised Marie, and she sprayed a little of her coffee into the air before having a short choking fit.

"Oh great," Dr. Heller said. "Another drunk. Didn't you learn anything from the last boozer you married? Should we save time and get the restraining order now?"

"Do you still go to those meetings?" Marie asked. "You haven't had a drink in ten years, since after your divorce."

"The meetings are comforting to me, Mama. Anyway, Jacob and I decided to get coffee after a post-meeting chat. One thing led to another, and we started dating. He is the gentlest spirit, seriously."

"Well, I hope he isn't some vagrant living on the streets," Dr. Heller said.

"Jerry!" Marie said.

"Oh Daddy, I told you he has a respectable government job downtown. He's been sober for years. Most people that go to A.A. aren't vagrants. Where do you get those ideas? Jacob lives in Oak Park, inherited a nice house from his parents when they passed a few years ago. Charming Tudor-style, the house isn't huge but it exudes character and style. It needs a little redecorating, a few nice finishes in the kitchen. When we marry, I plan to move into his place with him."

"Is he divorced?" Dr. Heller looked down his nose disapprovingly.

"No, Daddy. His wife died in a car accident several years ago. He doesn't have any children. Besides, I'm divorced. Who am I to judge? You aren't going to be a pill when you meet him, are you?"

"Your dad just wants the best for you," Marie said. "We both do. When are you thinking about getting married?"

"That's why I'm here. I have a couple of dates for you both to consider."

"Oh great!" Dr. Heller shook his head as he spoke. "Will I be paying for another extravaganza at the Palmer House Hotel?"

"No, Daddy. We plan to marry at our church. The one I've been attending with Jacob will be just perfect. You won't need to pay for anything. We're adults. Seeing as we are both in recovery, we plan to serve cake and punch at the reception, no booze."

Dr. Heller stared for a moment at Cynthia. "So, he's a religious nut?" He stood up as if preparing to walk out of the room.

"Daddy!" Cynthia threw up her hands in exasperation. "Mama, don't let Daddy dismiss Jacob out of hand."

Dr. Heller walked across the hall from the kitchen to his oak-paneled study. Marie and Cynthia followed.

"Dear, let's not judge the man until we have a chance to meet him at least." Marie walked over to her husband as he lit his pipe by the fireplace. She put her hand in her husband's and looked back at Cynthia. "I'll get the calendar out later and we can see what dates you are thinking about. We'd like to meet your young man and get to know him. Perhaps we can come to Chicago around Christmas for dinner and a show."

"Great. Now I'm on the hook for two trips to Chicago," Dr. Heller withdrew the pipe from his mouth and set it in the crystal ashtray on the mantel.

"I hope he'll come with me for Thanksgiving here, assuming we're invited," Cynthia said.

"You are always invited," Marie said.

"I'm going to lie down before supper. I find this all very tiring." Dr. Heller walked into the hallway, pausing at the bottom of the staircase to eavesdrop on his wife and daughter's conversation.

"It's a lot for your father to process, Cynthia," Marie said.

"If I told him I was gay or drinking again or any number of things, he wouldn't have batted an eyelash."

"It's the religion thing. You're right. Because of his job, he's always had trouble with the protestors and smug, self-righteous Christian types. I know all Christians aren't hypocrites. Your Jacob is probably a fine fellow. Give your father some time. He loves you very much, Cynthia. He loves you more than anything…even me, I suppose."

7

The moonlight cast strange shadows on the trees. Shanta hated the parking lot of her condo. It had been conceived as part of a planned community where everyone would walk, but a chronic shortage of parking places made her life miserable. After working late as a nurse at St. Anthony's, she had stopped by the all-night grocery. There never seemed to be a good time to get all the errands done. Shopping in an almost-empty store certainly sped up the process.

Just sixty yards from the side entrance, with her hands full, she sighed heavily and locked her Sentra with the remote. Shadows from the landscape lighting danced playfully behind the rows of parked cars. Shanta didn't love coming home late at night, but by now she'd grown accustomed to the routine. Feeling at home in the parking lot of her building, she never worried much about her own safety. Growing up in Chicago—now that was dangerous. Someone she knew got raped or shot or beaten up once a week in Cabrini Green. When her mom remarried and moved to Ohio, Shanta happily left her drug-and-violence-riddled high school. After graduation from Springfield High, she selected nursing school at a university within commuting distance. Her life fell into place.

Shanta's soft-soled shoes barely made a sound on the blacktop. She passed two suvs before something unusual caught her eye in the moonlight. A person-shaped shadow bobbed in and out behind her. *Oh no!* Her life-long fear involved being assaulted in a parking lot. She dropped her bags of groceries and tried to fish in her purse for mace.

Before she could get to the self-defense spray, she felt a wire pull taut around her neck, stopping her in her tracks. Shanta stood straight up, struggling to move forward. Instinctively, she dropped her handbag and brought her hands to her chin, trying desperately to pry the wire from her neck. The razor-sharp metal cut into the fingertips on her right hand.

Wanting to run or to call out, the garotte restricted her throat like a choker chain on a dog. The suddenness of the attack startled her, and now the pressure on her neck prevented her from screaming. Only a weak, barely audible squeal escaped from her throat. The killer slowly tightened the wire. She could feel the steel biting into her neck, choking off her oxygen supply. Battling the panic that engulfed her, Shanta begged for mercy with her eyes.

"Mother," she called out in a low, hoarse voice. "Help me!"

Her self-defense training proved useless. With mind and body flailing about, she finally remembered to stamp on her assailant's foot. Unfortunately, her expensive tennis shoe proved an inadequate weapon against the hard-toed boots of her attacker. She mule kicked and caught the shin of the assailant. Again, the wire tightened, causing her mind to grow fuzzy. Shanta kicked at one of the plastic bags of groceries, a last act of defiance. She watched a random can of corn roll away, following the gentle slope of the parking lot, then coming to rest after bouncing off a large tire on an Escalade.

Tighter and tighter, the killer constricted the wire around Shanta's neck. Finally, lifeless, she fell, to the pavement.

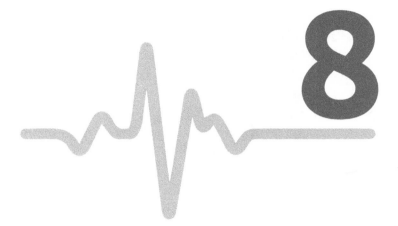

"What are you so serious about this morning?" Terrell's mother asked.

"Nothing, Mom," Terrell said, without turning around. He nervously zipped his gym bag—open and closed, open and closed—as their car drove down a side street.

"Terrell, please stop with the zipper. You are making me crazy. Are you sure nothing is wrong?"

"Just thinking about wrestling, Mom." Terrell said.

Exchanging glances with his father in the rearview mirror, Terrell just wished the ride to church would end. Being cooped up with his parents seemed unbearable. The whole family knew he was lying. They must.

The Benson's sedan pulled into the parking lot of the large, warehouse-like church building a few miles outside

Springfield. Like always, a brigade of smiling faces stood near the glass front doors. Two women held open both doors so Terrell and his family could enter. Part of the pastor's plan to rejuvenate the church, a large number of volunteers gathered in the lobby, greeting and directing first-time visitors where to go. Personally, Terrell hated the attention so early on a Sunday morning. The welcome brigade swarmed his family, attempting to make everyone feel like long-lost loved ones returning from war. *A bit much.*

Ashley and Marcella sat on a cushioned bench in one corner of the lobby. Terrell walked over to them, trying to look pleasant. Marcella rose first, hugging Terrell and smiling. There is the man of the hour. "You won again! State tournament, here you come." The smiling Latina, with sparkling brown eyes, greeted her best friend's boyfriend.

Terrell knew that Marcella's smile usually belied mischief that defined her character at school and church. Why did his Ashley have to be besties with the class clown? While Terrell liked Marcella on one level, she had a habit of making sarcastic remarks, trying to be funny. Her efforts, in any environment, rubbed him the wrong way. Her attempts at humor often led to trouble, and loose lips could turn his pregnancy problem into a disaster. He wanted secrecy and discretion, not a wise-cracking sidekick who might betray confidences at any moment just to get a laugh. What if she outed Ashley as pregnant and his parents found out?

"We meet again at the holy place, ladies," Terrell said, trying to sound like everything remained status quo.

"Hey, we beat you here," Marcella said. "Your dad drives like he's Amish."

"Best to be careful out among the English," Terrell said in his best Amish accent.

"Come along, pilgrims." Marcella responded. "Let's get to teen class."

The girls rose from their seats. When they stood, Terrell leaned in to whisper something to Ashley. "Why didn't you answer my calls last night?" Terrell felt irritation rising in his voice.

"My phone died. I plugged it in to recharge it and forgot to turn it back on." Ashley blushed a bit and scrunched her forehead. Terrell recognized this as a telling sign that she was lying.

"Let's just get to class, you two," Marcella whispered again, intertwining her arm with Ashley's. "You can duke it out after we learn about becoming better Christians."

The trio trudged upstairs to "the loft," a space specifically designed by the youth pastor to appeal to older teens. Dim lighting and comfy chairs welcomed them as they filed in and eyed their regular seats.

Two visiting interlopers occupied the bean bag chairs, usually claimed by Ashley and Marcella, so they reluctantly took two folding chairs next to Sarah Warren by the heavy, wooden coffee table. Ms. Warren, their affable facilitator, greeted each one by name. Terrell sat on the couch, at the far end of the room with the boys. He grunted hello to all as he sat down. Jason nodded in return.

Suddenly, waves of guilt began to roll over Terrell. Not just sex before marriage, now he and Ashley found themselves considering abortion. He needed to find a place to hide, and it wasn't in a Bible class at church.

"Welcome everyone." A widow in her early fifties, Mrs. Warren reminded Terrell of a beloved elementary school teacher who saved him from "new guy" anxiety years ago. Her graying brown hair and warm smile felt like a magnet to him. Once class started, she turned all business, trying to corral the teen minds into the confines of the Sunday

School lesson. She unfolded her gold-rimmed reading glasses and balanced them on the end of her nose.

"Thanks everyone for coming today," Mrs. Warren continued. "More than ever this week, the lesson requires your enthusiastic participation. This series of teachings is all about discussion and not just me blabbing at you. For the two new folks today, we are studying the book *Eight Curve Balls: The Bible and Modern Culture*. Feel free to jump into the conversation whenever you feel so moved."

Terrell's mind wandered. He knew about curve balls. How could he have gotten himself into such a mess? He understood the mechanics of birth control from health class, but things happened fast the first night he and Ashley went all the way. Only their third date, he asked her to a drive-in movie, expecting her to say no. She agreed and the evening progressed quickly, partly due to the boring movie. Lots of cuddling at first, then suddenly she unbuttoned her blouse to give him a peek.

Abrupt laughter from the class brought Terrell back into the moment. Like the night they went to the drive-in, Ashley looked just as hot this Sunday morning in her tight black jeans and turquoise blue sweater.

What were his parents always saying about taking responsibility? His future would be bright if Ashley just jettisoned this baby. That seemed like the responsible thing to do, but what if abortion isn't right in God's eyes? No one warned him about the moral dilemmas that come with creating a baby. Where did all this emotion come from? He hated emotion.

Terrell's intellect told him the expedient answer: the easy choice would be abortion. The heart painted a different picture. Deep inside, he longed to see his little baby, to hug him or her, and to care for the child. But he couldn't. No way. His parents would kill him if they found out. His dad would throw him out and expect him to get a job immediately. He had no money for such a decision. *Why did God let this happen?*

What about senior year? What about wrestling in college? This time should be the best year of his life, full of wrestling and cutting classes, not morning sickness and worry. A week ago, he walked around a carefree teenager. Now, he felt like a grown man with adult-size problems.

"Ashley, what do you think that Scripture means?" Mrs. Warren startled Terrell out of his thoughts.

"Oh, I'm sorry," she said. "I wasn't paying attention."

Marcella pushed the open paperback in her friend's direction and pointed at the Bible verse. Ashley stared at the words on the page. "For you created my inmost being; you knit me together in my mother's womb. I praise you because I am fearfully and wonderfully made; your works are wonderful, I know that full well, Psalm 139:13."

As Ashley read the words aloud, emotion kept building in her voice. At the end of the Scripture, her face drained of all color. Terrell wondered if she might faint. Then, his own nausea began.

"Okay. Stop right there," Mrs. Warren said abruptly. Although her tone seemed kind, her next words hit Terrell like a ton of bricks. "What does that Scripture mean to you, Terrell?"

Although he couldn't think, he didn't want to betray their secret to the class. He tried to form a response. None came out. How did Mrs. Warren know to make Ashley read the Bible verse? *Then, she asked me the follow-up question? That can't be a coincidence.* Marcella swooped in for the rescue.

"Well, it sounds like, apart from the biological facts about how a baby is made, God knows us in our mother's womb." A couple of the younger teens guffawed at her repetition of the word womb. "You know, God gave each of us special and beautiful characteristics, even before we pop out into the world. For example, he planned my gorgeous hair and killer sense of humor. Isn't that what it means?" Marcella patted her hair, then pointed both index fingers toward her mouth.

Mrs. Warren smiled at Marcella. "Very good, Marcella. Thank you. Pete, will you read Jeremiah 1:5. The teacher adjusted her reading glasses to follow along as Pete read.

Marcella smiled toward Terrell at the other end of the room, probably expecting a thank-you smile for the bail out. Instead, he responded with only a slight head nod.

"Okay. Let's see. Where is Jeremiah again?" Pete asked waving his Bible.

The other boys laughed as Pete fumbled through from the beginning of 66 books.

"Doofus, the verse is right there in the workbook," Marty said. "Page 42. Pay attention!"

"Oh, I see," Pete said. "Before I formed you in the womb, I knew you …" Marty again laughed at the word *womb*. "Before you were *born* I set you apart; I appointed you as a prophet to the nations."

"Pete, what do you think that verse means?" Mrs. Warren asked.

"It means God has big plans for us, even when we are in the womb." Pete smiled with self-satisfaction that he worked the word womb into the conversation one more time, causing Marty and another boy to snicker.

Terrell glared irritably at them both. *Immature freshmen,* he thought. Little did they know about the womb secret going on right now in their class. He couldn't believe that this lesson had to come up today. It felt like an interstellar conspiracy to make him go mad. Maybe God did it to punish Ashley and him for sinning? Frustration mounted. Although he wanted to avoid attention, a small tear formed in his left eye and dribbled down his cheek. He quickly brushed it off with his hand.

A teenager named Julie fielded the next verse. "Can a mother forget the baby at her breast and have no compassion on the child she has borne? Though she may forget, I will not forget you! Isaiah 49:15."

"That's right, Julie," Mrs. Warren said. "What do you think that one means?"

"Well, maybe God is comparing His love for us to the love any mother has for her baby. His love for us is never ending. I can't wait to be a mother." Julie beamed with pride.

Marcella shot back, "I can." The others laughed at her quick response.

Hearing those words, Ashley gathered her book and purse and stood up. Sobbing, she hurried out of the room. Marcella leapt to her feet and followed in hot pursuit.

"Is everything alright, girls?" Mrs. Warren called after them timidly. No one answered.

Terrell knew better than to follow. He forced himself to stay in his seat until class ended thirty minutes later. The lesson spoke to him and weighed heavily on his conscience. How could he make his parents understand? How would he convince Ashley to keep their baby? The rest of the class dragged on as he tried to think of a way.

"Okay everyone, that's it for today," Mrs. Warren said at last. "Get your money in if you want to come along to the bowling night next week. The cost is $10 per person. I need an accurate count to reserve the right number of lanes. Okay, enjoy the church service and have a good week."

Terrell caught up with the girls in the courtyard. Marcella sat on a concrete bench without a jacket, apparently immune to the cool, late autumn temperatures. Ashley stood nearby, not talking, her hands jammed in the pockets of her cheerleading jacket.

"Terrell, what is wrong with this girl? Did you cheat on her? I will punch you in the face if you cheated." Marcella put up her dukes as if to box Terrell.

Ashley stood silently. She shook her head no. Marcella looked back and forth from Terrell to Ashley and back again. "Well, somebody tell me something."

"If I let you in on a secret, you can never, ever breathe a word to anyone," Ashley began.

"Ashley, I'm not sure this is a good idea," Terrell said.

"Shut up!" Ashley nearly shouted in Terrell's direction.

"Ash, absolutely," Marcella said. "I will never tell a soul. Cross my heart and swear to die. Did you guys go all the way? Is that what this is all about? Feeling a little guilty, you two? I'll bet Terrell pressured you after the football game the other night. Everything always happens after the football games. Why do they even play that sport in high school? It's a veritable Sodom and Gomorra in that parking lot on Friday nights."

Terrell shot Marcella a death stare. He doubted Ashley's choice to let another person in on their secret, particularly Marcella the Mouth. His girlfriend would do whatever she wanted to do. He had no say in the matter—no say in anything. She might as well get it over with. Nothing to do but stick around and try to mitigate the damage.

Marcella waited impatiently, shifting on the stone bench. Terrell stared at her in disgust for a few minutes as Ashley composed herself.

"I am going to explode if you don't spit it out," Marcella said.

"Okay, here it is straight up. I'm pregnant. Terrell's the father."

"Oh my goodness, oh boy!" Marcella said looking aghast.

"I didn't see that one coming."

"Neither did I," Ashley said.

"Neither did I," Terrell added.

"You are telling me you have a little bambino growing inside of you right this moment? A real, live, human baby? My best friend is with child."

"Yes, that's what I'm telling you," Ashley said. "In my womb."

Terrell winced as she repeated for dramatic effect the word overused in class.

Marcella jumped up, took two giant steps toward Ashley. Then she hugged her with all her might. Losing her balance, Marcella almost caused both of them to topple into the dormant rose bushes. Composing herself, she backed up a step and stared at her friend's tear-stained face.

"Ashley, why are you crying? This is about the coolest thing I have ever heard. Isn't it? You're going to be a mama. Oh, wait. Your parents… Oh!" As if she just remembered that others might have opinions and thoughts, Marcella finally quieted down.

"Right." Terrell said. "This isn't going to be smooth sailing by any stretch of the imagination."

"Have you told your parents?" Marcella asked, addressing both of them.

"No." Terrell said. "We need space to make some decisions. So, don't go blabbing to anyone at school. The last thing your best friend needs is everyone snickering at her behind her back."

Marcella hugged Ashley aggressively once more. "This is just wonderful. Not that you haven't told your parents. You are going to be a mommy and a great one, I bet."

Terrell stared at Ashley's face as she hugged Marcella. Eyes open, she seemed to be sending a message with her facial expression. Terrell couldn't decipher what she meant.

"Maybe," Ashley said. "Maybe, I will become a mom."

Marcella sat back down. She turned and looked toward Ashley. "Oh. I forgot about that other possibility. Of course, you have to explore all the options."

"I already saw some people," Ashley said. "You know, people that take care of this kind of problem."

"Oh, Ash." Marcella looked sad and stared hard at the statue in the courtyard. "I hope you don't go that route. You can handle parenthood. My parents are doing it, and they aren't the brightest lights in the Milky Way."

"Yeah. Think about it. Terrell doesn't have a job. I don't have a job. We both want to go to college. We both have dreams, but maybe not dreams that go together. Heck, we don't graduate high school for another six or seven months."

Marcella just stared at her friend. Then, she said the inevitable type of thing she would say. "Well, I love you. No matter what you choose, we are sisters to the end. I will be with you through this whole thing."

Ashley started to cry again. The door opened and an older lady hurried past the three friends while heading toward the parking lot beyond. Once the door glided shut and the woman hobbled far enough away, Terrell pleaded, "Marcella, please don't say anything to anyone. Ash needs you."

9

Detective Lawson stood over the body as a Level III CSI lifted the sheet. Not unfamiliar with death, Lawson's eyes scanned the entire corpse from head to toe. The African-American woman's face appeared purplish-blue. She wore scrubs, probably a doctor, nurse, or other healthcare worker. Her eyes bulged, and the eyelids remained open. A significant amount of blood had leaked from the right side of her neck and only now started to congeal. Same as the woman in the park, wire marks encircled the victim's neck. The pink scrubs seemed undisturbed with no sign of rape or even significant struggle.

A uniformed officer walked up behind Lawson. "Hello, Detective Lawson. I was first on the scene."

"Hi, Ted. What do we know so far?" Lawson asked.

"African-American, 31-year-old female, her name is Shanta Greene. She lived here in unit 314 with her mother and child. They expected her home last night. Sometimes emergencies come up. The victim might have to work a double shift at the hospital without any advance warning. The mother didn't get worried until this morning and hadn't reported her missing. We found Shanta's car way over that way. CSIS dusted it for prints, and they are towing it back to the garage. No sign of struggle readily apparent from the car. Looks like the victim was carrying a bunch of groceries when she was attacked. The building has a couple of security cameras, one at the front entrance and one by the side door. Neither camera shows a good view of this area specifically, but I asked the manager to email all footage from last night to the SPD detectives email address."

"Probably coming home from work, stopped for groceries. Someone either waited for her, or she was just in the wrong place at the wrong time," Lawson said. "When CSI is done, you can release the body to the morgue. I'm going to go up and talk to the mother."

Walking through the lobby, Lawson saw nothing remarkable. Mailboxes lined the left wall and a sofa grouping hugged the wall to the right. He copied the manager's phone number from a sign by the vacant front desk. Most interesting, two older-looking security cameras perched above the lobby: one directed at the entrance and another facing the mailboxes. *Perhaps the security cameras caught something helpful for a change.*

After knocking on the victim's apartment door, an attractive fifty-something woman answered. "I'm Detective Lawson with Springfield P.D. I realize you've been through a lot this morning, but I really need to get as much information as possible. Can we talk?"

"Yes, I'm Shanta's mother, Maxine. Come in and sit down. Charles, go in your room. I need to talk to this man."

A young boy, five or six years old, looked up from the game he had been playing on a tablet. He trudged past the couch where Lawson sat with his grandmother.

"I told the patrolman everything I know. We expected her home from work last night about 12:30 a.m. The boy and I had gone to bed. Sometimes, she works over if they are short staffed. She doesn't call me because it would wake us up. When I got up this morning, she still wasn't here yet. It didn't particularly worry me until the young man knocked at the door."

"Do you know anyone who is mad at your daughter, an ex-boyfriend perhaps?" Lawson asked.

"No, I've really tried to think," Maxine said, scratching her head. "Shanta parted company with Charles's father years ago when she first got pregnant. He wanted no part of that responsibility. To my knowledge, she hasn't heard from him. Since then, she's hardly dated—spends most of her time at home with us when she's not at work. There was a man, good-looking guy that she went out with a few times last spring. I don't think anything came of that."

"Do you happen to know the man's name? We are just looking for any lead that might get us closer to finding who did this to your daughter."

Maxine put her head in her hands. Lawson wondered if she was crying. After a pause, she looked up and said, "I don't remember his name if I ever knew it. You might try looking in her phone."

"Do you know if she used a code to get in her phone? Otherwise, we might have to wait for a couple of months to get a warrant and get the phone people to let us into her records."

"Her code is probably 0914," Maxine said. "That's her

birthday, and she used it for every PIN and code as far as I know."

"Thank you, ma'am," Lawson said. "Here is my card. If you think of anything else that might be helpful, just give me a call. I promise you we will do everything within our power to find the person responsible and get justice for Shanta. When we make an arrest, I'll let you know. I appreciate your time."

10

Madison loved being alone in her kitchen early in the morning. The coffee maker gurgled, sending rich aroma throughout the house, announcing that a new day awaited. Just outside the front door, she heard a newspaper flop up on their big front porch. Before long, the kids would wake up and start talking chattering to each other in their low morning voices. Zane would hear them and jump in the shower. Soon, everyone would pile into the kitchen. But for these few brief moments, she savored the perfection of coffee, the quiet, and a fresh morning.

Setting the newspaper on the island, she stared down at the blaring headline: SECOND WOMAN MURDERED IN SPRINGFIELD. The apartment complex where the woman lived wasn't far from the clinic. Madison scoured the news story for details. Unfortunately, the newspaper couldn't answer the main question on her mind. Why?

After scanning the rest of the headlines and a quick look at the weather, she poured two tall travel mugs full of Fair-Trade Black. Outside, chipmunks dashed around hiding nuts and playing tag. The brick patio and gardens, now covered in a very thin blanket of new snow, reminded Madison that she still needed to rake a few leaves before winter fully set in. How would Zane react to the major news she planned to share this morning? She had a good idea, but no certainty. Lately, he seemed happy that their two kids were getting a little older. "Less bother," he had told her.

"Good morning, hon." Zane waltzed into the kitchen and planted a quick peck on Madison's cheek.

His not-yet-buttoned sleeves exposed curly black hair on his forearms. Madison stroked his arm and patted his back. "I'm always amazed at how fast you can get ready."

"It's one of my super powers," Zane said smiling. "It facilitates that extra ten minutes of sleep every night. Without that ten minutes, my life would be torment."

Madison smiled at his dry sense of humor. "Big day today?"

"Living the dream: another day of teaching history to a bunch of high schoolers. Then, the team wrestles Tecumseh High. It's an away meet, which means I'll be at least thirty minutes later than usual. Best of all, I get to come home to my perfect wife and family."

"And don't you forget it," Madison said, smiling at her hunky husband. She reached in for a kiss, ignoring her lipstick. *Working out with the team so often, his six-pack only gets better with age,* she thought as she lightly stroked his stomach. "I have a little news for you."

"What's that, babe?" he asked absentmindedly while patting his pockets to see if his keys were in his pants.

"It looks like the perfect family will be increasing in size next year. Doctor Heller says another munchkin is heading our way."

Zane looked stunned at first, but quickly broke into a big smile. "Really?"

"Would I lie?"

He repositioned his body and hugged Madison enthusiastically. Her kisses tasted like cream and coffee.

"That's amazing news," Zane said. "Do you feel okay? Are you more tired or anything?"

Madison loved when his paternal instincts kicked in. "Yes. Doctor Heller thinks everything looks fine. I feel okay … a little minor morning sickness. That's why I checked with Heller, well, that and a home pregnancy test. The doc approved me for gestation."

The two hugged and Zane aggressively kissed Madison one more time. She responded, feeling his body press close to hers.

"Hi, Mommy!" Shelby announced her arrival into the kitchen.

The spell of the moment was broken in an instant. The couple quickly unclenched their embrace. "Hi sweetie. How is Braden? Is he awake?"

"How should I know? Am I my brother's keeper?"

Madison wanted to correct Shelby for the precocious remark, but just didn't have the heart to spoil the moment with Zane.

"Yes, Shelby," Zane said. "You need to watch out for your brother. If he falls and breaks his noggin, your mother and I will have to spend all our money fixing him. Then we won't have any money for Christmas presents in a couple of months. Wouldn't that be sad?"

Shelby scurried to the other room to check on Braden. Madison stared at her travel mug and tapped on the counter.

"Are you sure you feel okay?" Zane asked. "You look pensive."

"Just wondering if we are adding a boy or girl. Do you care which one?"

"My preference is healthy and happy. We can trust God that it's just the right little addition to our family."

******

Terrell waited in front of his house as Ashley pulled up in her Mustang.

"Hey, Ash. How's it going this morning?"

"I'm okay. What did your parents say?"

Terrell shifted in his seat to look at Ashley. "Well, they had a cow. My dad called me a 'ho hopper.' My mom cried and said that I'd messed up my life despite every advantage they gave me."

"What did they say about paying for the procedure?" Ashley asked.

"They said they will pay—if that's what we decide."

"I don't even understand how that will work? I'm not their child. Will their insurance pay or do they have to use their own money?"

"Look, I don't know anything about insurance. My parents will figure out the financing for the abortion. If you feel ready, call that woman from the clinic. Ask about the insurance rules if it makes you feel better? Money doesn't need to be the main thing here. Are you positive we are doing the right thing?"

"What do you mean, Terrell?"

Ashley's face grew taught, and Terrell could sense another argument or crying session building. He couldn't help continuing his train of thought out loud. "That lesson at church in the teen class got me thinking. We are literally ending a little life that maybe God intended to be born. If Mrs. Warren is right, God knew that kid before we even conceived it. I just feel like slowing down and taking a minute."

"Why do you do this to me?" Ashley asked. "Bringing up these questions doesn't help. I'd cry again right now, but my mascara will run all over my face. Besides, I'm cried out. Last night, it took forever to fall asleep. I just laid there in the dark, and tears ran out of my eyes for hours. My parents know something is going on. I'm acting funny, and they can tell I've been lying to them. They ask me over and over what's wrong."

"You are just trying to spare your folks the pain," Terrell said. "They would thank you if they understood. Call what's-her-name from the clinic and see how much money we need to bring. I will go with you this Saturday."

Ashley pounded the steering wheel. "I'm not sure what to do. You are having second thoughts. I'm confused. Once we go through with it, there's no turning back. I'm supposed to be a Christian, Terrell. Does faith mean anything in this situation?"

"Okay. I hear you, but I can't decide for you. I don't want to talk about it right now. If I'm late for homeroom again, I may not get to wrestle tonight. Let me out over there." Terrell jumped out of the car at the entrance to the locker room. He didn't kiss Ashley goodbye, as was their custom.

He just grabbed his gym bag and bolted. *Sweet*, he thought. The locker room door stood ajar. The custodian probably propped it open to air out the smells after he mopped. Terrell liked to drop off his bag at his locker before school. This saved him a trip back across campus at the end of the day.

As he peeked in the open door, the coast looked clear—
no one around. He walked slowly through the mostly
darkened room. A single emergency light and the red
glow of the exit sign provided just enough illumination.
He easily found his locker and dialed the combination in
the dim lighting. As he opened the metal door, he thought
he heard a sharp sound behind him. Quickly wheeling
around, he saw no one. The dark and empty locker room
unnerved him.

After stowing his gym bag, he closed up the locker
fast and started toward the stairs. Just as he reached the
corner of the landing for the stairwell, a large figure almost
mowed him down. Terrell screamed and the other man
let out a sound that eventually formed the word, "What?"

"Oh, Coach Matthews, it's you." Terrell exhaled with
a giant whoosh.

"Terrell, you almost scared me to death," Coach Matthews said. "What are you doing down here with all the
lights off."

"Sorry, Coach. I just needed to drop off my gym bag.
It's a long run from my last class of the day to get back
to my school locker and then over here for wrestling. So,
I like to pre-position my bag when I can."

"Oh. Well, that's sounds smart, son. Have a good day
at class. See you down here before we leave for the meet."

"I'm stoked. Ready to kick butt." With that, Terrell disappeared up the steps and headed for his first class.

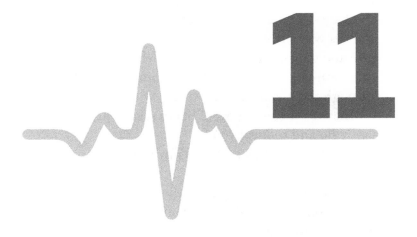

11

A woman, wearing a cream-colored coat, stood near the fence as Madison pulled her Volvo into her regular parking place. She noticed that the lady had a much dressier appearance than the four men carrying anti-abortion placards while trudging up and down the sidewalk, chanting "Love your baby." Madison could tell the lady wanted to speak to her, but Madison wasn't in the mood for a lecture about life beginning at conception or abortion stopping a beating heart.

The woman waved to Madison and motioned her to come to the fence. "Hello. My name is Sarah Warren. Can I talk to you a minute?" Madison noticed the woman's coiffed black hair and expensive shoes. She had seen a similar pair at Nordstrom's when shopping with her mother.

Her first instinct was to run to the door of the clinic, but this well-dressed woman intrigued her. Curiosity about the lady's calm and inviting demeanor made Madison wonder why she wasn't shouting like the others. Her kind face and glowing green eyes lured Madison to the fence. After walking the short distance from her car, she smiled through the metal structure at the woman.

"Thanks for coming over," Sarah said. "I just wanted to say hello and to meet you."

"I'm Madison. I work here. Why did you want to meet me?"

"There's something special about you. I pray for you every Monday. Sometimes, I wonder why you work here? You could work at a hundred jobs, I'll bet."

The question made Madison irritable. "I wonder about you too. Why would anyone spend their valuable time harassing women who need medical services, not to mention the service providers? You look out of place here."

"Good question. Maybe, I love the women and want something better for them. Or maybe I love the little lives inside the women. How did you decide to take this job?"

Suddenly, a man came running up behind Sarah Warren.

"You are killing babies!" he said. "Stop murdering the unborn. God sees what you are doing."

"Alright Luis," Sarah said. "You made your point. This young lady and I are speaking."

The man turned and walked back toward the sidewalk.

"Who was that?" Madison asked.

"His name is Luis," Sarah replied. "He's harmless, at least I think so. Luis is a bit wound up because his niece had an abortion last month, over in Columbus. What were you about to say?"

"I care about women too and don't want them butchered in a back alley," Madison said, feeling her cheeks flush. "Young women need help, someone to take care of them. We offer valuable services. The shouting and yelling at us and our clients won't do any good, you know. Women still make the right choices for their individual situation."

"We all have reasons for what we do. The men over there who do most of the yelling—they strongly believe they are trying to stop a holocaust of sorts." Sarah's face filled with emotion, as if desperately wanting to convey some subliminal message. Madison couldn't discern the underlying secret, if there was one.

"Do they now?" Madison asked, hoping Sarah caught the sarcasm in her words. "It sounds kind of nuts to me."

"Next Saturday, a noisier bunch of protestors are coming over from Morris Chapel. I wanted to warn you. They're harmless, but the volume will go up considerably. Don't be afraid."

"Oh, I never work Saturdays. I have a young family and want to be home with my husband and children."

"So, you're not here on abortion day?" Sarah asked. Madison could see the wheels turning in Sarah's head.

"No. Look, I'd better get to work. Thanks for trying to be a person at least. It goes a lot farther than the boisterous mob behind you. There is something different about you. We should have coffee sometime. Maybe I can share a few facts about what we do."

"That would be great," Sarah said, smiling warmly. "I stop for coffee at the Starbucks on Grange Hall Road almost every weekday in the afternoon. Come by sometime around one p.m. if you can. I'm usually there typing on my laptop for an hour or so."

Madison didn't answer yes or no; she just smiled and turned toward the clinic. Once inside, she tried to hurry past Vanessa, but no such luck.

"Good morning," Vanessa said.

"Hi, Vanessa. Is Madge in yet?"

"No. She didn't see you fraternizing with the enemy in the parking lot. Madge is at the dentist this morning. Root canal. She will be out all day. Relax and enjoy the morning."

Madison moved her hand across her brow and let out an exaggerated sigh. "I forget about the security cameras in the parking lot. This woman Sarah, one of the protestors, wanted to meet me."

"I set some files in your office for the appointments today. You only have two ladies scheduled so far, one at 10 a.m. and one at 2 p.m. They both filled out the forms online. Be sure to follow up with the appointments from last week. Madge will kill you if you don't get at least a couple of procedures booked for Saturday. Speaking of killing, did you see the news about the new murder?"

"I saw the paper this morning."

Vanessa stood up and leaned over the welcome counter. She spoke in a hushed tone even though the two women were alone in the office. "I recognized the name and picture of the first victim. Becky Holcomb was a client of ours. Remember that unusual mole on her chin? And look at this woman, Shanta Greene, is also a former client."

Vanessa set the newspaper down on the counter. Scanning the picture, Madison tapped the newspaper. "Oh, yeah, I remember her now that you mention it. She eventually chose to have her baby, I think. Nurse, with no man in the picture."

"Yes. She worked at St. Anthony's," Vanessa said. "I heard from my hubby that Holcomb was a regional manager for some bank. She chose to live in Springfield because it's in the middle of her territory. Didn't know a lot of people, but Phil met her at the gym. Apparently, she liked the same type of elliptical machine. Per Phil, she seemed super athletic and did cardio for close to an hour. How do you suppose someone caught up to her to kill her? The attacker must have been mighty speedy himself."

"Slow down, Vanessa. Maybe the victim wasn't running when the killer grabbed her? He might have tripped her on the running trail? Or maybe he got her to stop with some kind of ruse. Who knows? Whatever, I hope the cops get the creep soon. You and I don't jog, but Zane takes the kids to that park sometimes. Just thinking about it is making me anxious. I better get on making those calls. These abortions don't schedule themselves."

Madison walked to her office and fired up the computer. Following her routine, she turned on the Keurig, inserted a coffee pod, and refilled her travel mug. Hanging up her coat, she looked out the window through barely open blinds. Sarah was standing in the same spot where they had talked, her head bowed. She was probably praying. Two of the men twirled their placards and chanted some slogan barely audible through the thick glass. Madison clicked on an Internet radio channel, and soon, background music filled the air, covering any noise from outside.

The song playing reminded her of her mom. What on earth, Madison wondered? After almost a year working for Planned Parenthood, she suddenly started thinking about God and her mother's disapproval of her career choice. Under her breath, Madison prayed for the first time in a long time. "God, if this job isn't right for me, give me a sign. You know how dense I can be; make it a clear sign that I need a different job. Amen."

The list of emails on her screen included one from Madge Abzug. Madison read the message first: a reminder to make the follow-up calls from the previous week. The email caused Madison to grind her teeth. Why couldn't Madge give her a little credit? She knew what to do without being prodded. The first thing she learned at the clinic: Follow-up closes the deal.

The first name and number on her list was Ashley Featherstone. No answer, as expected. The young woman would be in high school at nine in the morning.

Madison left a message: "Hi Ashley, this is Madison from the Women's Health Center. I'm just calling to see if we can be of further service to you. If you need anything at all, please give me a call. I will check back with you later. Just want to make sure you are okay and answer any questions." The next number belonged to Stephanie Jordan. Her intake interview went well, but three weeks had passed and no appointment for a procedure. "Hi, Stephanie. This is Madison from the Women's Health Center."

"Oh, yes. Hello."

"I'm just following up to see if we can be of further service to you? Have you made a decision?"

"Yes," Stephanie said. "I guess I have decided to have the procedure."

"Excellent," Madison said. "We have a couple of openings for this Saturday. Does that work for you?"

"Oh, I suppose so. Do you have an afternoon appointment? I don't get up too early. I work late on Friday nights."

"Honey, that's no problem. Can you get here by 1 p.m.?"

"Yes."

"Very good. You can have the 1 o'clock slot, no waiting. Remember to bring identification and your insurance card. When you arrive, pull into the same parking lot. A volunteer will walk you from your car to the office. We'll take good care of you."

"Okay. It's settled then. I will be there on Saturday at
1 p.m."

"Very good."

Sometimes her job made Madison feel like a used car
salesman. *Just six more abortions sold and I can win a free
toaster. Madge will be pleased.* Madison dialed through
the rest of her list, fifteen names and numbers. Only two
women made appointments for Saturday. Three is the
minimum because at least one person usually cancels at
the last minute or just won't show up. According to Madge,
the doctor gets cranky if he comes out to the clinic and
doesn't have at least two procedures to bill.

The morning dragged by as none of the others on her list
called back. The only scheduled walk-in client cancelled.
Madison spent a lot of time perusing the Internet—never
too early to start Christmas shopping. At lunchtime, she
warmed up her Lean Cuisine meal in the microwave.
Vanessa came by to chat for a few minutes, then headed
out for a meal with her sister.

At 1:30, the doorbell rang. Madison remembered Vanessa wouldn't be there to buzz in any clients. The woman at
the door looked frightened and disheveled. After stepping behind the desk to buzz her in, Madison greeted
the young woman at the door and showed her where to
hang her coat. When she removed it, Madison noticed
her pronounced baby bump.

Although not unprecedented in her time at the clinic,
Madison seldom met with women as far along as Dee
Brooks appeared. "There's some paperwork we will need
for you to fill out, but you can do it while we talk. Come
back to my office. I'm Madison. May I get you a coffee
or a water or anything?"

"Water would be great. My name's Dee."

After retrieving a water bottle from her mini-fridge,

Madison sat down next to Dee. "So, what brings you in today?"

"Thanks for the water. Well, I'd like to know if I can still get an abortion here."

"Dee, I will be glad to go over the options with you. The short answer is probably. How far along are you?"

"The doctor says I'm at 23 weeks."

"How long have you been considering terminating your pregnancy?"

"Not too long. I already have two rug rats. I just found out today that my lying, cheating boyfriend, Javid, is sleeping with another woman. He doesn't care about us. The last thing I need is a third baby with no daddy to pay child support."

"Well, the abortion choice is entirely yours. At your stage of pregnancy, we recommend some additional precautions before and after the procedure. Are you willing to go through a couple of extra steps, including a medical exam?"

"Whatever it takes," Dee said with her voice trailing off. "I just can't take this life anymore. Javid's not kind to me. Perhaps it's guilt or maybe he's just not the guy that I thought he was when we met. Why does this keep happening to me?"

"Dee, let's slow down for just a minute. Let me understand your situation. Have you had previous abortions?"

"Yes, a couple. Both happened before I met Lance and before I had the two girls. Just like all the rest, both baby daddies eventually dumped me and moved on."

"Are finances an issue?"

"You bet they are. Javid and I are barely making ends meet. Lance hasn't paid child support since Javid moved in. I'm taking Lance to court, but my lawyer says that could take months. How will I feed another mouth, not to mention diapers and all the other hoopla?"

"We have a program to help with the cost of your procedure. You just need to fill out the paperwork. You probably can get your pre-care and your procedure for free if your household income doesn't exceed $26,000. Does that assistance sound like something you may want to apply to receive?

"Yep," Dee said. "Just give me the forms and sign me up. Let's get this thing out of me as soon as possible."

Madison stood up and went to the file cabinet. She found the appropriate financial assistance forms for Dee, as well as the required intake form and waivers. "You can sit at this credenza over here. Fill in everything you can. I will be right here at my desk, and I can answer any questions you have along the way."

Dee rose, moving from the desk to a chair at the credenza. Once seated, she began filling out the forms. Due to her baby bump, Dee sat sideways next to the writing surface.

Madison smiled, remembering logistical challenges during her own pregnancies. She enjoyed carrying both of her children to term, but she recalled the inconveniences, great and small. As the thoughts about her own children flooded in, a splitting headache descended from nowhere. She pressed her right temple with her forefinger. The pain diverted a bit, moving to the back of her head.

"What does primary insured mean?" Dee asked.

Trying to fight through the pain of a gathering migraine, Madison replied, "That would be you, honey. However, you mentioned that you don't have insurance at the moment? Is that right?"

"Yeah. I lost my insurance when my job at Sears ended. My ride share company doesn't offer benefits."

"Okay, just put in your personal information. In the

next section, it will ask about insurance. Just write 'none.' That's all you have to do for that part of the application." After she spoke, Madison turned to look out the window. For some reason, looking at Dee's pregnant body made her want to throw up. Her headache throbbed to the point Madison thought she couldn't stand much more. Headaches this severe rarely bothered her. This one felt like a man in combat boots tap danced into her day and onto her skull. The middle drawer of her desk contained Tylenol, but her migraine meds remained in the medicine cabinet at home. She fished the bottle from her desk and quickly downed two caplets with a big swallow of coffee.

While Dee worked through the form, Madison could hear shuffling about in the outer office. Vanessa must have returned from lunch.

"Where do I have to sign?"

"Let me show you. There are three places for initials and one for your full signature." Madison got up and walked to the credenza. Using her own pen, she put small check marks next to the appropriate blanks on the form.

Within minutes, Dee signed up for her free abortion, complete with pre-op and post-op care. Madison smiled through her headache, knowing that Madge would be super excited. Madison handed Dee off to finish up the scheduling. Although she would have preferred to go home and lie down, she soon began counseling another young woman with a baby inside.

With the interview barely begun, Madison's phone rang. This was unusual, as Vanessa usually held all calls during client appointments. "Yes?" Madison asked.

"Madison, sorry to disturb you." The voice on the other end sounded like a woozy baritone. *Madge must be slurring her words following her root canal.*

"Hello boss. Are you okay? How can I help?"

"I know you are with someone, so I'll make it short. The dentist found another problem with my teeth. He has to perform a second root canal, and he can't do it until Friday. He says my mouth will hurt like crazy. I'm going to be needing major pain meds. The problem is that the pills make me feel loopy. I just can't work. Bottom line is that I need you to come in on Saturday."

"Oh," Madison said, lacking her usual cheerfulness. She was thinking about losing time with Zane and the children. Although she usually guarded her weekend time, this seemed like a good reason to make an exception. "I understand. What hours should I plan to be here and what will I do?"

"I hate to ask it because you specifically try to avoid working weekends, but there is no choice really. Vanessa can't man the front desk and assist the doctor. Confirm with her when you need to arrive at the clinic on Saturday."

"Wait! You want me to assist in a procedure?" Madison could feel her headache spike along with her blood pressure. "I'm not a medical professional." *Why would Madge ask such a thing?*

"Oh silly, you won't be doing surgery. You just stand around and get the doctor anything he needs. For the most part, he will just want you to hold the wand for the ultrasound. I can walk you through it on Thursday when my head clears a little. Vanessa tells me you scheduled three procedures for Saturday. That's great. Remember, no cancellations!" Madge's voice took quite an unusual journey up and down in pitch as she said the word *cancellations*.

Madison smiled at just how high her boss sounded on the pain medication. "No cancellations," Madison repeated.

"Thanks for helping out, doll. I really need you to do this for me."

The line went dead. Madison didn't remember saying yes, but Madge signed her up for a front row seat to three abortions. This would be a new step in her women's clinic adventure. She wasn't looking forward to it.

12

"Stretch out my hamstring more," Terrell said. "It feels tight and I don't want to pull a muscle this close to the tournament."

Lifting Terrell's leg off the mat, Scott picked up Terrell's heel and extended his leg to vertical. "Keep it straight and tell me when," Scott said. Then, he slowly pushed the leg beyond ninety degrees.

"Okay, hold it there a minute," Terrell said.

"Did you hear about that murder over the weekend? We used to ride skateboards down that trail."

"Yeah, the news anchor got all preachy about personal safety and how the police should have solved both murders by now."

Scott lowered Terrell's right leg and picked up the other one. He repeated the same process on the second leg. "Tell me when."

"Okay, right there," Terrell said. "My dad suspects it's someone from another town. He says people don't just start killing right and left. They work their way up to it. Then, they keep doing it until they get caught."

"That sounds right, but how does your dad know that kind of thing? Doesn't he work at an electronics shop?"

"He knows stuff. He's glued to the television and watches real-life murder shows all night sometimes. You know, cops solve a real crime with camera crew in tow. We watch together sometimes. I might go into criminology. Some of that stuff is fascinating."

Suddenly, a whistle blew and all the wrestlers stopped what they were doing and gathered in a half circle around Coach Matthews. "Okay guys, I want to see some real sweat today. Take four trips around the gym and then line up for movement time. Jason, you can lead us today."

Moans ensued as the wrestlers reacted to his words. The team began jogging around the gym, gaining speed as they went. A familiar face headed toward the coach.

"Hi honey, why are the wrestlers groaning?" Madison asked, walking up behind her husband.

"Babe, I wasn't expecting you! But always a pleasure. Movement time is our name for a sort of calisthenics where one person leads and everyone else mirrors the leader's movements. Jason is one of the lightest wrestlers, so he is able to move back and forth faster than the heavier guys. If I pick him, the big boys know they will be working hard during this part of practice."

"Zane, I stopped on my way home because I have something to ask you. The clinic needs me to work Saturday. Did you have any big plans? Can you stay with the kids, or do I need to ask my mom to sit with them?"

"We don't have a meet Saturday or anything. I can change practice time to Sunday afternoon. No problem, my sweet."

"You are a lifesaver," Madison said while pecking Zane on the cheek. "Madge never asks me to work, but she's recovering from a root canal or something." Madison didn't want to tell Zane about her new duties on Saturday. He would not be pleased. They'd had all the discussions about Planned Parenthood she cared to have with him.

"Are you taking off or do you want to watch practice for a while?" Zane asked.

"I might hang out for a few minutes to see you whip them into shape," Madison said. "Then I have to pick up the kids." As she walked toward the bleachers, she heard Zane's whistle blowing again.

After the wrestlers finished their movement session, they ran over to the mats and broke into pairs. "Okay, first we are going to practice leg sweeps. Our takedowns were pathetic last week. You have to find ways to get your opponent off his feet. You know the moves we've been practicing; use all of them until something works. We can't win consistently without mastering takedowns. At the whistle, go!"

In a moment, action began all over the gym as pairs of wrestlers worked on takedowns. Every few seconds, a body would hit the mat with a thud that unnerved Madison. Her headache flared up again with the noise and body slamming. As the wrestlers heated up, the smells in the gym also increased. In the midst of the seeming chaos, a fist fight erupted on the mat closest to where Madison sat rubbing her temples.

Zane looked up from writing in his notebook. He rushed over to the mat where Terrell and Tank were throwing haymakers at each other. Blowing his whistle, he stepped between the two and barely dodged a wild punch thrown by Terrell. A small trickle of blood oozed from Tank's nose onto his upper lip.

"This is wrestling practice, not boxing. Terrell and Tank, give me forty trips around the gym. Now!" The two wrestlers started running laps with Terrell quickly opening up a sizable lead. "The rest of you get back into pairs and practice sit outs."

Madison watched the two young men run laps. Zane watched her face light up as if she suddenly put two and two together. This must be Ashley's Terrell.

******

As practice ended, Coach Matthews approached his star wrestlers. "Tank, you hit the showers and then come and sit outside my office. I want to hear both sides of this story. Terrell, you first. Let's go to my office now."

Coach Matthews walked downstairs with Terrell in tow. They entered the coach's office. Terrell slammed the door after them. The glass rattled in the metal door.

"Take it easy on my door. Okay, what started the fight?" Coach asked in a calm, but commanding voice.

"Just a little misunderstanding between teammates, sir."

"What was the misunderstanding about? I don't want to be here all evening sorting this out. As you could see up in the gym, I have a beautiful wife, and she wants me home for dinner."

"Tank said something he shouldn't have said. He needs to know I'm not afraid of him."

"Terrell, you can't get baited into silly fights. You are going to end up getting thrown out of school for something stupid. High school guys make dumb jokes all day long. Do you understand me? If you want to fight every time another student says something stupid, you are going to be in trouble constantly."

"Coach, I take a lot from him, but he can't talk bad about my girlfriend."

"Terrell, I know you feel added pressure. There is no need for you to take anything extra from anyone. I won't stand for any racist comments at all. You know I will come down hard on inappropriate racial stuff. I will kick guys off the team, but standard dumb comments are part of being a teenager. Look, you are a very promising wrestler. Your whole life is in front of you."

"I used to think that, but not anymore."

"What does that mean?" Coach Matthews asked. "What's going on all of a sudden? You seemed on top of the world a week ago. You are likely to be in the state meet in a few weeks. What's bringing you down?"

"If I tell you something, will you keep it a secret."

Coach thought about the request. "Terrell, as a teacher, I'm legally bound to report specific things, like sexual abuse or if a crime has been committed. But generally, I don't betray confidences. What I will promise you is that I have your back no matter what. I'm not a gossip. I would only repeat what you told me if it is absolutely required by law or school policy."

"Tank was ragging on my girlfriend."

"That's not the behavior I expect from a teammate, but you have to control yourself. A lot of good men have lost everything by giving in to jealousy."

"The girl I'm dating says she's pregnant." After a long pause, Terrell continued. "We only just started having sex a little over a month ago. I thought I used protection, but it must not have worked right. Now, neither of us knows what to do."

"Have you told your parents?'

"No, Coach. How can I tell them? They will be so disappointed in me. Worse yet, I told my girl that I did tell them. My future is all my folks talk about. Since I was nine years old, Dad has been lecturing me about not getting involved with girls before marriage. We go to church. Dad will hate me. Things seem so out of control. Ashley's already been to an abortion place."

After a pause, Coach looked Terrell square in the eyes, "Terrell, you are a fine young man in a lot of ways. I am not happy that you lied to your girlfriend. Wrestlers don't lie. We do make errors in judgment sometimes. This pregnancy issue constitutes a mistake, but it doesn't have to define you. What matters now is how you respond to the problem."

Coach Matthews looked compassionate, and Terrell looked like he might cry. "Uh huh," Terrell said with a gulp.

"First, you need to grow up fast. You've gotten yourself into an adult-size problem, so you need to respond like an adult. Problems can be solved, but you can't lose your head and do something crazy. Second, you need to stand by this young woman. Although you should have a voice, it's her decision about how she proceeds. You can't force her or pressure her into doing something she doesn't want to do. I don't like abortion, feel like it punishes the baby for mistakes the parents made. Even so, there is no way I'd think any less of you or your girlfriend if that's the choice she makes. It's not my job to judge anyone else but me."

"Everything became so real so fast, too real for me right now. I feel like a kid. Being a father seems like a huge step."

"It is," Coach Matthews said. "Having a baby is one of the most important things you will do in your life. This pregnancy affects both of your families. You need to tell your parents soon and encourage Ashley to tell hers as well. Then you need to decide together how best to handle the pregnancy."

"Oh, we can't tell her parents. They'll go crazy. Her dad might kill me."

"The young woman needs medical attention. That requires insurance. There are risks whatever path she chooses. She has to tell her parents. They have a right to know about a situation with these long-term implications. Abortion can have long-term affects physically and mentally. Obviously, bringing a child into the world would also have huge consequences as well."

Neither said anything for a while. Finally, Terrell got up to go. Coach shook his hand and opened the door for him to leave.

"You can talk to me anytime. Go on. Get out of here before the other guys start coming down for their showers."

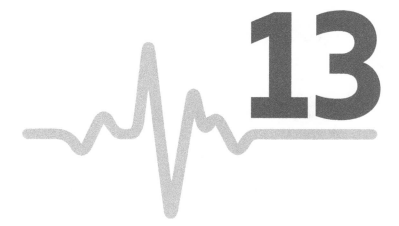

The voice on the other end of the phone used many words, but said very little. The sound quality rated marginal at best. The raspy made the called almost sound like they were speaking a foreign language. Detective Lawson scribbled notes, patiently waiting for the caller to stop talking. As nearly as he could tell, the woman on the phone saw someone hanging out near the jogging trail at the park. She saw a man who "looked Hispanic" near where the first strangled woman's body turned up.

"Okay, could I ask a few follow-up questions?"

"Let me call you back," the anonymous voice said. "My boss is coming, and I might get in trouble for doing this on company time."

With that, the line went dead. Detective Lawson banged his fist on the desk. How many incomplete or unreliable tips would he entertain for this strangler case? Feeding reward information to the local evening news channels and interviewing the grieving families always results in tips. Few of them amount to anything worthwhile, but every credible one requires man-hours to follow up. Public relations disasters result when police fail to follow up on leads.

"Any good tips yet on the strangler case?" Detective English asked.

"Not really," Lawson replied. "Some Spanish-looking guy supposedly hanging out at the park near where the first victim was found. Before I could ask any questions or get a better description, the caller claimed her boss was coming, and she *had* to get off the phone."

Lawson continued to scour an on-line database, looking for another strangler who used a garotte. The most recent homicide occurred two years ago, way over in New York City. Police suspected a certain organized crime figure or one of his henchmen. Why would the mafia in New York care about the mundane affairs of Springfield? Wasn't Ohio a little beyond their field of play? The next most recent strangulation using a wire occurred in Chicago five years ago.

Lawson faced another night of little sleep and much worry. The heat from the Chief of Police wouldn't end until they came up with a suspect. Two women killed within days of each other and not a single clue.

******

Hearing loud banging upstairs, Marie Heller set her coffee mug on the kitchen table.

"What's going on?" Cynthia asked, emerging from the

guest room.

"It's your father. He is probably having one of his nightmares. I'd better go check on him."

A loud, guttural scream wafted down from above. Marie quickened her steps up the staircase and hurried to their bedroom. Throwing open the door, the scene looked like pure madness. Jerry stood on their bed, wearing only his pajama bottoms. His hefty stomach stuck out considerably. With fists closed, he pounded hard on the wall and repeated the same phrase: "I will get you, you little wiggler."

"Jerry!" Marie called out in a loud voice. Her husband ignored her and continued to strike the wall with his closed hand. As she drew closer, she saw him aim at specific flowers in the wallpaper pattern. "Jerry!" she shouted even louder.

He paid her no mind until she climbed up on the bed and put a hand on his shoulder. In an instant, her touch broke the spell, and he opened his eyes. "Marie?"

"Yes, honey. it's me. What is going on?"

"Was I dreaming?" Jerry asked sheepishly while stepping down with a thud. He sat on the bed. "It seemed so real. They were everywhere. I had to kill them before they took over everything. It was just a dream though, right?"

"Well, dear. Of course, you were dreaming—a nightmare truth be told. You're awake now, thank goodness. Get your shower and come on down for breakfast. You will be late to the office."

As Marie turned to leave the bedroom, she saw Cynthia standing by the open door. Shooting her a warning look, Marie descended the stairs almost as quickly as she'd gone up.

Opening the refrigerator, she took out a can of biscuits, a carton of eggs and a stick of butter. On her way to the counter, she turned the oven to preheat while juggling the contents in her hands. Cynthia entered and sat on a barstool at the kitchen island. She watched her mother butter a glass pie pan and begin arranging raw biscuits for baking. "Like some coffee?" Marie asked.

"Sure. Do you have any creamer?"

"Your dad and I take it black, but I think there may be a can of condensed milk in the cabinet." Marie hunted through the bottom shelf of the cabinet near the stove. "There it is." She pulled a manual can opener from the drawer and opened the milk for Cynthia. She then poured coffee into a large, red mug.

"Does Dad have those dreams very often?"

"Cynthia, your father has always been a heavy sleeper. Don't make too much of a silly nightmare." Marie placed the biscuits in the oven and collected a pan from the lower cabinet to fry the eggs.

"I'm not making a big deal, but that abortion business must take a toll on his mind. His two jobs have diametrically opposed purposes. As an obstetrician, he works to bring healthy new lives into the world. He took an oath when he became a doctor to do no harm. Then on weekends, he murders a baby or two or three. Over time, the contradiction must do something to a person's psyche."

"Stop it. He doesn't need you trying to analyze him. Jerry's always done the best he can to provide for this family. Besides, a lot of ladies in this town couldn't have gotten a safe, medical abortion without him. No telling the butchery that might have taken place. Believe me, his abortion patients don't share your new-found reservations about our livelihood. It's all more complicated than simply choosing life or death."

"Mom. I'm not judging Daddy. I'm really not. Look at what a mess I made of my life before Jesus: the drugs, the booze, two failed marriages. The last thing I would do is judge anyone. Grace is out there for anyone who wants it bad enough. Daddy's changing. It's not just the nightmares. He looks different. Something bigger is going on, something in his mind. That's all. I'm worried about him. Don't you see that he isn't acting the same?"

Marie put down her utensils and stifled a sob. She grabbed a paper towel and turned away from her daughter. Cynthia got up from her stool and walked over to her mom, putting her hands on her shoulders.

Without turning around, Marie said, "Cynthia, maybe something is wrong with him. Who knows? I try not to notice, but the little things add up. His mind appears to be playing tricks on him. He never used to get angry about anything. Now, he flies off the handle at the least little thing. The other day, he had a strange episode in the shower. I heard him calling out and thought he might have fallen."

"Oh, Mama."

"He was sitting on the bench in the shower just talking like there was somebody else in there with him, but there wasn't. He looked at me with the strangest expression, like he barely recognized me. I'm worried that he is losing his grip on reality."

Marie opened the oven door to peek at the biscuits. Satisfied with their progress, she put the eggs in the pan and turned on the gas burner. Then, she hurried to the refrigerator and took out pre-cooked turkey bacon to warm in the microwave.

"Has he seen a doctor? You know, has he been professionally evaluated?"

"What do you think?" Marie asked.

"Either he refuses to go or he gets a buddy to tell him he's fine."

"Jerry reminded me in no uncertain terms that he is the

only doctor he needs. He refused to make an appointment. Doctors make the worst patients."

Minutes later, Jerry descended the stairs. The two women became quiet as he joined them in the kitchen. Before the three of them dug into their breakfast, Dr. Heller leaned over to smell a stunning bouquet of yellow roses setting on the large island. "Did you cut them this morning?" Dr. Heller asked.

"Dear, it's much too late in the season for roses like these. I got them at Oberer's."

The look on Cynthia's face troubled Marie more than Jerry's comments. She set the orange juice on the table. "Come on, let's eat while it's hot." Marie thought as she savored a long piece of thick bacon.

"Marie, you have outdone yourself. The biscuits are perfect. Everything's delicious."

"Thanks, dear. Cynthia may have had a good idea about a cruise next year. After we get through the wedding and all, let's take a little cruise to the Caribbean. What do you think?"

"Anything is possible," Dr. Heller said. "I think we might enjoy a summer cruise to Alaska. Last time, weren't we kind of hot at the ports of call in the Caribbean?"

"That sounds good, Daddy," Cynthia said. "Alaska would be great for you two. Is there any way you can give up just part of your practice? Maybe let go of the abortion end of things and just go part-time as a gynecologist?"

"Or maybe take on a partner?" Marie asked. "You talked about selling your practice someday when you retire."

"Cynthia, again with the abortion thing? These Christian nuts have done something to your sense of reason. What about a woman's right to choose? Do you ever think of that end of it?"

"What about the baby's right to choose?" Cynthia just

stared at her father. "Who is sticking up for the little lives that are cast aside to line the pockets of Planned Parenthood."

Marie could see the wheels turning in her husband's brain. Then, his expression turned eerily cold. A blank look covered his entire countenance. He didn't say another word during breakfast. He just chewed his bacon and mopped up the rest of the egg yolk with a delicious biscuit.

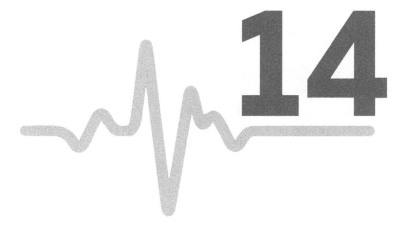

14

Terrell hated family picnics. To him, the whole black family reunion thing seemed like a blast from the past that should have stayed in the past. He didn't even like half the people who filled up their large backyard. The only bright spot, besides the food, was the unseasonably warm November day. Otherwise, everyone would have been scattered around inside the house. The downstairs finished basement was large, but not large enough to comfortably accommodate this many people.

Relatives from all sides of Terrell's family gorged on barbeque sandwiches, three-bean salad, chips, dips, potato salad, and deviled eggs. The smorgasbord represented torment to a wrestler in mid-season form. His father's three sisters sat in a semi-circle under the large oak tree, gossiping about this one's new girlfriend or that one's handsome boyfriend. Woe to anyone who didn't measure up to his aunts' standards for one reason or another. Terrell's mother had little to do with them, calling them the Fire Aunts. She'd had her own run-ins with their stinging comments long before she married into the family.

Worst, Terrell hated the political discussions. Same old ideas and same old lack of progress. They argued about issues that must be fifty years old. When would someone fix these age-old problems?

"Terrell, come over here and sit with the menfolk," Gerrard said. "You need to get in on this discussion. We need the younger generation's perspective."

Reluctantly, he picked up his folding lawn chair and set it next to his uncle. Gerrard always made things interesting. He probably represented the only Republican at the gathering of at least sixty-five people, at least the only one bold enough to admit it. Terrell's grandfather labeled Gerrard everything from an Uncle Tom to a traitor to his race. Gerrard always kept his cool and acted respectfully to everyone. The classy attitude was not returned by most.

Terrell admired Uncle Garrard's composure and his willingness to state unpopular opinions, but he didn't think his uncle correct about the ability of free enterprise to fix generations of inequity.

"Today's history lesson is about Margaret Sanger and Planned Parenthood," Gerrard said.

"Oh goodness no!" Terrell's father responded. "Here we go again. Terrell, be ready to go get the garden hose. This could end badly."

"Hear me out now," Gerrard began. "At the beginning, Margaret Sanger wanted to use abortion to thin the herd of black babies. In maternalistic fashion, she knew that all us poor, black children would just end up on drugs, committing crimes, and being a drag on society. Her thinking—and that of most Democrats at the time: Isn't it more compassionate to just end these misbegotten lives in the womb?"

"Maybe she had a point when it comes to little Republicans," Terrell's father quipped.

"Think this through with me. The wife of a KKK leader hatches a plan to use eugenics (like Hitler used) to abort black lives. It worked so well that Planned Parenthood has now killed one-third of all black fetuses in the United States since Roe v. Wade. Doesn't this bother anyone but me?"

"It doesn't bother me that women who can't keep their legs together end their pregnancies before they pump out an endless number of welfare babies they can't support," Terrell's father said, while two of the other men applauded and cheered.

The words cut Terrell. He looked at his father with a new contempt he hadn't felt before. Ashley is not a welfare mama. Quite the opposite, her family is on the upper end of society in this one-horse city. The two of us are just kids.

"Hold up," Gerrard said. "People make mistakes. That's true, but what about the ripple effects of abortion. There is a reason so many young women black and white run from relationships. The guilt and regret don't do anything to cement relationships or marriages. The fallout for men is equally destructive. By terminating pregnancies, men find it easier to move from woman to woman, instead of being drawn into a relationship commitment."

"Gerrard, I love you, but you are dead wrong," one of the cousins said. "Less abortions would just mean more poor kids growing up without fathers in their lives."

"That's right," Terrell's father said. "Just look at the mess over in some of those neighborhoods on the west side of Dayton. Shootings every night! It isn't safe to drive through there, let alone raise a family there."

"I don't agree," Terrell said. "Crime has to do with poverty. It isn't a result of too many families: single parent or otherwise. If I got a woman pregnant, I wouldn't abandon the kid regardless of whether or not the mother wants to get married."

At first, silence followed his comments. All eyes turned to Terrell. His father stared daggers through him. The other men in the circle of chairs began to offer catcalls and indicate their trepidation at the expected reaction. Terrell's father stared daggers through his son.

"Boy, what do you know about being a father or an adult? You couldn't find your way to first base with a woman if you had an umpire directing you. On top of that, you know nothing about having a job or supporting a child. Just keep your opinions to yourself until you are old enough to have a family of your own."

The words slipped out before Terrell could think, "Maybe I am old enough to have a baby, Dad. Maybe my girlfriend is pregnant right now, and we are having your grandchild."

Terrell rose and stomped off toward the food table. He didn't hear the comments behind him, just a lot of murmuring. In a few minutes, his father joined him.

"Son, do we need to have a talk? For real?"

"Dad, I wouldn't know where to start. I'm in a mess."

"Well, get your mother, and let's go in the house," Terrell's father said.

"Right now?" Terrell asked. His father's facial expression told him to go get his mother.

Doing as told, Terrell quickly found his mom in her bright yellow sundress. Although she didn't want to leave the picnic, she followed him into the house.

"Back here," Terrell's father yelled from the door of the downstairs guest room. When Terrell and his mother entered, his father patted on the bed for his wife to sit down with him. "Our son has something important to tell us."

"Couldn't this wait until our guests are ready to leave?"

"Mom, Dad, I should have told you this before. Ashley and I were trying to figure out how to handle this ourselves. Oh, this is hard."

"Spit it out, son," Terrell's father said. "Don't beat around the bush."

"Ashley is pregnant," Terrell said.

"No way," his mother responded. "Are you telling me that you got that cheerleader trash pregnant with your child? What is wrong with you?"

"Look, it wasn't planned. We haven't even been having sex that much."

Both parents laughed caustically, and his mother rolled her eyes. His father couldn't sit still any longer. Standing up, he began waving his arms and pacing as best he could in the small room. Terrell sat down on the chest at the foot of the bed to keep from getting run over by his father walking back and forth.

"What do you plan to do about his situation you've gotten yourself into?" his mother asked.

"That's just it," Terrell said. "Ashley is talking about an abortion."

"Sensible girl," Terrell's dad said. "You two have no resources, no education."

"She went to the women's clinic in town, and plans to have an abortion next Saturday. The thing is ... that I'm not so sure."

"Are you out of your mind, son," his dad said. "You have

no money, no job, no plan. How are you going to support a wife and child? Let the girl get the procedure, break up with her, and chalk this up to life experience."

"Dad, you've taken us to church all these years. Now, we come to a problem, a real moral dilemma. You want me to forget everything we've learned at church."

Shouting, Mr. Benson said, "Where were all these Christian morals when you were humping like an animal in your girlfriend's sportscar?"

Mrs. Bunsen stood up and walked over to where Terrell sat. She put her hand on his shoulder, looking off into space. "Son, do you realize what's going to happen if she doesn't get an abortion," she started gently, but morphed into something angrier. "About six months after the child is born, you will be working your minimum-wage job. Life will be very difficult. You and this girl will start arguing and hating each other. You will break up. Then, she will sue you for child support. For eighteen years, you will pay her every month or the law will come and lock you up in jail. Any chance you had at college will be gone because you have to keep working fulltime to pay the child support. You are ruining your life."

Terrell didn't know what to say. He stared at his parents, who both looked at him in uncharacteristic ways. His father looked so disgusted with him. His mother's face belied pity tinged with judgement. Neither had ever looked at him with such condemnation.

"I think our son needs to think about this," his mother said. "I need to get back to our guests. Let's all take some time and cool off. We can talk about this more tonight."

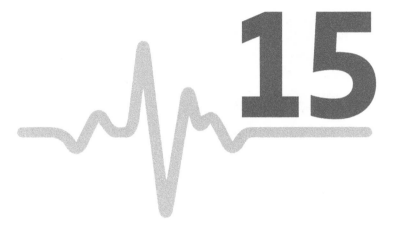

15

Terrell drove his parents' sedan toward the fenced parking lot of the Women's Health Center. Luis stood on the sidewalk right next to the driveway screaming like a madman. His sign depicted a mass of body parts in a bloody collage. "Don't kill your baby! Stop before it's too late. Don't do it!" His energy and rage spilled over and bumped the car with his sign.

Ashley cringed as she saw the sign and recoiled from the wild man shouting. Terrell eased through the gate, guarded by two volunteers in yellow vests. He parked near the front entrance, as far as possible from the fence and the protestors. A third volunteer, also wearing a vest, walked quickly to their car. The gray-haired man smiled and greeted Ashley and Terrell, then hurried them inside the building. Despite the older man's best efforts, both heard the chants grow louder. Almost at a fever pitch, the protestors chanted louder and louder, ready to lose control as they realized another little one moved toward certain death inside the clinic. Terrell glanced back over his shoulder just in time to see an overwrought young man run toward the fence. Banging into it with his hands, he screamed, "Don't do it!"

Once through the outer door, Terrell looked at Ashley. She appeared rattled by the raucous crowd. The escort knocked once on the inner door, and Vanessa buzzed them in.

"I can check you in," she said. "Good to see you again. We will need your photo identification. Are you going with insurance or direct payment?"

Terrell produced his father's credit card as Ashley handed over her driver's license.

After finishing up at the desk, the couple found a place in the corner of the small waiting room. They sat holding hands, staring at the boring landscape picture on the far wall. Terrell tried not to think about what would come next. Only one other lady sat waiting; she didn't seem nervous at all. Terrell tried not to stare at the woman's baby bump. His mind didn't like the imagery of a baby growing inside this woman now, but likely floating in a container an hour from now. Next time he saw her, she would no longer be pregnant. The child would be so much trash. His fight-or-flight instinct told him to grab Ashley's hand and run out of the clinic.

"I'm so glad you came along," Ashley said.

"No problem, baby." Looking at the time on his phone, Terrell shook his head. "We are super early."

Madison opened the waiting room door and smiled

at Ashley and Terrell. Then, she focused on the woman with the baby bump.

"Dee, you can come on back."

Minutes later, Madison reappeared and walked toward Ashley.

"Hi," Ashley said as Madison approached.

"Hi, Ashley. And this is?" she asked, even though she remembered seeing Terrell at her husband's wrestling practice.

"Oh, this is Terrell," Ashley said. "He came with me today."

"Pleasure to meet you, Terrell. It's going to be about an hour before we get to Ashley. Vanessa will help if you two have any last-minute questions. Magazines are over there. Just try to relax and don't worry. We will get to you as soon as possible."

*****

Sitting nervously back at her desk, Madison tried to think about anything to take her mind off assisting the doctor. Soon, she would be called into "The Room." During the week, the door to the Procedure Center always remained closed. In Madison's mind, a steel curtain separated her office from the locked room down the hall. A little squeamish about blood anyway, she rationalized her avoidance. Details of any medical procedure grossed her out.

Her own abortion included general anesthesia. Never having seen an abortion, Madison only knew what she'd read in Planned Parenthood literature or heard from Madge. She wished it could stay just a vague concept. Apparently, her luck was about to run out. *Time to grow up fast.*

An unfamiliar face came to Madison's office door wearing scrubs. The mask made the woman seem more mysterious than warranted by the situation.

"Hi Madison, I'm Natasha." The tallish, dark-haired woman spoke in an emotionless alto voice. Her eyes appeared vacant.

"Good to meet you, Natasha. Do you want to show me what I will be doing?"

"Sure. There is not much to it. We just need one more set of hands. The doctor likes to use an ultrasound for later term procedures. It's for safety. The picture helps him know for sure what's going on. You will stand next to me and move the ultrasound wand over the woman's midsection and lower abdomen as he instructs you. Otherwise, your responsibilities are few. I will be handing him instruments and assisting. The other person in the room does anesthesia.

When we are done with this patient, we need to quickly get ready for the next procedure. We may ask you to help a little with clean-up as we turn the room around for the next woman. You can find an extra smock in the storage closet next to the director's office. Put one of those on. Be sure to get a mask too. If you have any trouble, I can help you tie it or whatever you need."

"Sounds simple enough," Asley said, though she doubted her own words. The comforting thought at the moment: she would focus on Dee's stomach and the video monitor. Ashley had experienced several ultrasounds during her own pregnancies and watched one of her friend's as well. Not much to it—her role in the procedure would be easy.

Once in her mask and gown, Madison indeed needed help from Natasha to tie on her surgical apron. That part of the process seemed fun, in a way. Her mom might be proud of her, almost looking like a doctor. Well, that was a stretch, she reminded herself. Mom would be on her knees begging Madison not have any part of helping with an abortion. The thought of her mother's pleading face caused a shudder. Guilt streamed in and she tried to think of anything else. Up until now, Madison had maintained a strict agreement with her conscience. You don't bother me and I won't drink alcohol to excess. Suddenly, all bets were off. As soon as this exercise in abortion ended, she planned to have a three-merlot night.

Any courage Madison built up ended when she headed back into the abortion procedure room. Dee lay on the table, looking vulnerable. Her I.V. had not fully kicked in. The apprehensive look on Dee's face stoked Madison's own misgivings. She squeezed Dee's hand and assured her everything would be alright. The anesthetist monitored the patient's vitals and asked her to count backward. Out of the corner of her eye, Madison could see a tall figure enter the room.

"Oh, Madison, this is Dr. Heller," Natasha said.

Nearly fainting, Madison turned to see her own gynecologist walk up to the operating table. All she could muster was a nod of acknowledgment. For security reasons, Madge never told Madison who performed the abortions. Alerts and sirens went off in Madison's head. Not precisely sure why, her doctor's presence seemed unnatural. The man who nurtured and helped her birth two healthy babies stood at the foot of the abortion operating table. In moments, he would extinguish the life of Dee's child, fetus, tissue, whatever.

Like a train coming down a track at 60 miles an hour, Madison saw no way but to stay on board. Oh, how she wished she could run out of the room and never come back.

"Okay, let's get that little wiggler pried out of there," Dr. Heller said.

His words sounded harsh to Madison, out of character for the kindly small-town physician she knew as Dr.

Heller.

"Fire up the suction," Dr. Heller said with unnecessary glee while picking up the suction device and another instrument. "Widen the cervix a little more, nurse. Madison, you can put some gel on the victim's belly, and let's start scanning. I need to see what's going on in there."

Hearing her name wrenched Madison out of her nightmarish trance. The surreal scene felt like nothing she'd ever known. "Yes, sir." She liberally squirted gel on Dee's abdomen, probably too much by half. As she placed the wand in the center, a picture broadcast on the screen directly in front of Madison, trying not to stare at the perfectly formed little boy floating in a sack of fluid. He almost seemed to be waving at Madison, trying to make contact. *Stop it!* Madison screamed at herself inaudibly. He's just some tissue. It! It! It! Not he, it.

"There's the little booger," Dr. Heller said. "I will have him cut up and out in no time."

Dr. Heller first inserted a metal device, at least that's how it looked to Madison on the ultrasound. Sensing the foreign object, the fetus moved away from the instrument. Madison didn't know what to think. She'd been told the baby felt nothing throughout the procedure. The doctor began cutting into the flesh of the baby's leg, causing the child to recoil—as if in pain. The device sucked the tiny limb toward the opening and the doctor manually pulled it out. He tossed the little limb into a waiting metal tray.

Madison felt she might lose consciousness. Beyond any horror movie she saw in college, this scene truly frightened and shocked her to the core.

"Score one for the old doc," Dr. Heller said jovially.

Natasha giggled at his remark.

"Now, we are committed," Natasha joked. "I'm sure mama wouldn't want a boy with just one leg."

"At least we don't have to worry about this lady cancelling on us," Dr. Heller said. "We are in deep."

Madison felt like she was in so deep she might drown spiritually. The callousness more than just rubbed her the wrong way. Heller's words grated against her brain and shaved tissue from her heart. The words and events she witnessed were permanently scarring her soul. How could this be the same man who delivered her two children? Panic threatened to overcome her. She needed a glass of wine. Suddenly, Madison didn't feel safe. Her own fetus might be in danger. Dr. Heller examined her just a few days ago. This butcher got so close to her child, the little life forming inside her body.

"Why do these women keep letting this happen to them? Over and over, they come for my help. If they could just show a little self-control. Maybe invest in a little birth control once in a while."

"Don't ask me," Natasha said. "I know we've seen this lady before. This must be her second or third abortion. She probably doesn't care if she gets pregnant. She can always come down here for a quick procedure."

The misogyny in Heller's voice sickened Madison. Natasha sounded just as jaded. They know nothing about the patient's situation. Madison did the intake and knew Dee's backstory. She's a real person with a life and people who love and depend on her. Suddenly, Madison wanted everyone to know the real Dr. Heller. If only women could see inside this room and the atrocities performed, Heller might retire and save a few lives.

Another wicked thought intruded. What if Dee could hear the doctor right now? Stories about patients waking up during operations make the rounds all the time. Just as this thought occurred, Dee mumbled something. The anesthetist checked one of the monitors.

Fortunately for Madison's stomach, the procedure took only about twenty minutes. The worst horror show she could have imagined unfolded in less time than it takes to watch a sitcom.

"Well, one more welfare baby saved from a life of degradation and crime," Dr. Heller said as he stripped off a latex glove. "This town should give me a medal. You girls clean up. I'm going to go eat my tuna sandwich before we start round two."

Madison could barely move her hands. She lifted the wand and mercifully ended the haunting picture of Dee's now-empty womb. Madison's head felt numb. No, her whole soul and body felt numb. She wondered if this stroke victims felt these sensations. She shuffled her feet to make sure they still moved. Had she personally ever felt so empty? Maybe after her own first abortion …

"Okay, all you need to do is empty that metal tray into the red plastic bag over there," Natasha said. "It's for medical waste. Then rinse the pan out in the metal sink in the janitor's closet right through there. When you are done, just leave the pan in the large plastic tub. A cleaning service picks up our reusables and sanitizes them."

The words seemed to flow from Natasha's mouth faster than Madison could comprehend what the woman said. She moved toward the metal pan, but could feel her stomach churning in a disconcerting way. Heller's words about the little wiggler haunted her. Then, she looked down to see the "meaningless" tissue which looked an awful lot like a dismembered fetus.

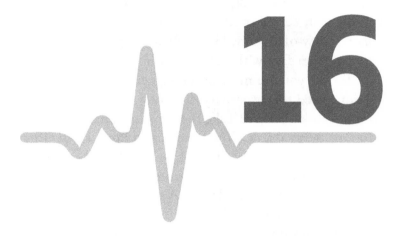

In the lobby, Terrell gazed at Ashley's face. "You look so sad. Are you sure you want to go through with this?"

"Terrell, I'm not sure about anything. But if we hang in there for another hour, this whole affair will evaporate behind us. We can go back to being two high school teenagers in love. Don't know about you, but I need that fresh start."

"Ashley, I love you. You know that. Once this is done, we can't undo it. You need to be 100 percent sure. If you need more time, let's wait a week. I'm sure you can come back next weekend, and they'll do the thing then."

Terrell looked over at the front desk and noticed a large man reading from a folder and eating a tuna sandwich.

The smell of the fish reminded Terrell of home. His mom made him tuna salad when he was trying to cut weight for wrestling matches. The older guy in the white lab coat seemed to be listening in on their conversation. Shifting in his seat, Terrell tried to position himself to block the man's view of Ashley. He stroked her golden hair and touched her face with the back of his hand.

"Terrell, you are making me so nervous," Ashley said. "I don't need this negativity right now. Why don't you go for a walk or a drive? Take the car. Get some food. Stop for an energy drink. Come back in an hour. I will either be done with the procedure or almost done. You can be right here for me when I come out."

"No, I'm sticking beside you. A real man wouldn't leave his woman at a time like this." Terrell slumped back in his chair, resigned to the situation. He played with his phone and worked hard to think of something else to say.

The door to the back office opened. Nurse Natasha helped Dee to one of the outer office chairs. Before she sat down, Dee stumbled a little and plopped onto the seat. Groggy looking, the still-half-sedated woman stared at Ashley as if trying to tell her something from the other side of a great chasm. The nurse returned back through the door where they entered. Suddenly, Dee slumped forward and appeared to be staring down at her shoes. A few minutes later, the smallest amount of blood dripped onto the floor in front of Dee.

Terrell and Ashley looked at each other. "I think I'm changing my mind," Ashley said. "Let me talk to the receptionist." With that, Ashley got up and walked over to Vanessa.

"Hi hon, how can I help you?" Vanessa asked.

"Um. I think I need to reschedule. Can we do this next weekend instead? Suddenly, I'm not feeling too well."

"Oh, Miss Featherstone, I'm afraid you can't cancel now. You would have to pay for the procedure as if you'd had it today. The doctor is already here, and we've set aside time in the operating room. The clinic incurs a lot of expenses whether or not you actually go ahead with the abortion. If you are having second thoughts, Madison can talk with you. I'll page her. Would you like to speak with Madison?"

The man with the half-eaten tuna sandwich slammed it down in the paper wrapper, then angrily tossed the mess into a waste can nearby. "Not another cancellation," he said caustically and stalked back to the inner offices.

Before Ashley could think of any response, Dee keeled over and landed on the floor headfirst. Terrell shot a worried glance in Ashley's direction. The two of them bolted for the door and ran to the sedan. Terrell burned rubber and sped out of the parking lot. Although she thought she could handle the procedure without telling her parents, Ashley now wanted her mother more than anything else on earth. She wanted to cry and to be held for a very long time.

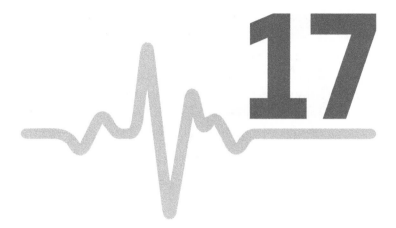

17

"Baby, here's your gin and tonic." Marie set the glass tumbler on a coaster next to her husband.

"You are a lifesaver, doll," Dr. Heller said. "Did Cynthia get back to Chicago all right?"

"Yes. Traffic must have been lighter than normal. Her text came at least a half hour before I expected it. Your baby girl really does love you. Don't worry too much about her newfound Christian beliefs. She's always been a joiner. I'm sure she didn't mean to send you on a guilt trip. It's like any new fad for her. A month from now, she'll take a yoga class or something, and we'll never hear the end of whatever new nonsense interests her. I do hope this Jacob guy turns out to be a keeper. I just want her to settle down and find a happy life."

"I'm not sure you are right about her getting over Christianity very fast, but she is our daughter. She will always have my love, second only to you, Marie."

The two sat in silence a few minutes, looking out the windows of their large music conservatory. The dog hustled out from below the grand piano and jumped up onto Marie's lap. She stroked the miniature dachshund's coat.

"Oh, Toby scared me," Dr. Heller said. "Wait, when did Toby come back? She died. Didn't Toby die?"

"Dear, Toby did die, years ago when Cynthia was a little girl. This is RBG."

"Oh, yes. Now I remember."

Marie looked at her husband, then said, "There's that deer again, Jerry, the one I saw last year trying to get water out of the pond in January. The design of white fur on its face looks exactly the same. I'm so glad she made it through the winter. I wonder how old she's getting."

Dr. Heller peered more earnestly out the window from his overstuffed leather chair. "Do you think *I'm* going to make it through the winter, Marie?"

"Oh, my dear, you'll live a long time. You're so active— but are you feeling ill? I told you to go see a doctor about those spells. We should call next week and get you in for a full physical."

"Slow down. It's hard to know what's wrong with me. How do I figure out who to start with if I were to get an examination? The last thing I need is a week's worth of tests only to learn that no one can figure out what ails me."

"Doctors sure do make the worst patients," Marie said. "How did it go at the Women's Clinic today?"

"Another nightmare day. The inept anesthetist didn't fully revive our first patient before sending her out to the lobby. Patient number one passed out in front of the young woman who should have been our second patient. Instead, patient two canceled, sending me into a mini-tirade. It made me furious at everyone. I can't tell you why exactly. All the indecision—it's so unnecessary. A fool could see patient number two is a high school girl, totally not ready to have a baby, particularly with a black man. They went so far as to schedule a medical procedure, then they talked each other out of it—with help from the bungling anesthetist. This inconveniencing everyone at the clinic must stop. It happens over and over."

"By this point in your career, you should expect last-minute cancellations. Abortion is a big decision. Women shouldn't make the choice lightly. I see how it's unfair to you though. You give up your Saturday mornings, and then these girls change their mind at the last minute and leave you hanging."

Marie looked at the man who had shared her entire adulthood. What did she see? A good husband and provider, he wondered. Maybe she saw someone off his rocker. He couldn't worry about that now. Still, the world offered him so much work to do.

"Twenty years ago, I wish I'd set aside Saturdays for golf. Do you remember when that doctor from Planned Parenthood HQ called on me. He was so persuasive. All the good I'd be doing for women and even society in general …"

Marie looked into his dark eyes. "You *have* done a lot of good. This town would have been so much poorer, much more crime-ridden without you. Don't give up just because a random schoolgirl cancels now and then."

"It just makes me so angry when they back out. Usually, they come crawling back a week or two later—all while I waste my time. They don't care about me or the other staff. Everyone in this world is selfish all the time. Young people scream at the old to get out of the way. Older people want everyone to give up their lives and become caretakers. The poor blame the rich and the rich blame the politicians."

"Oh dear," Marie said. "Is the world really that bleak?"

"We were supposed to have three procedures today, and we only had one. Between the religious nuts outside and other noise in the culture, women overthink abortion. If you ask me, many more young women should terminate their pregnancies. Everyone wasn't cut out to be a parent you know. If a single mom can't afford children, better to end the misery now than pass the suffering on to another generation. That's what ghettos are made from—broken dreams. Most women are ruining, not only their lives, but the lives of their little ones. If you don't have a stable family, why purposefully bring a kid into the world to screw the little thing up?"

"There's more to life than finances," Marie said. "You hear all the time about kids rising above their background. That's what my Rotary Club meetings are all about. I'm not sure all babies would agree that it's better not to exist."

"Now you sound like Cynthia," Jerry said, swirling his drink in his glass. "These aren't babies yet, they are just a bunch of rapidly growing tissue. Are you abandoning science too?"

"Oh honey, I love you. I'm the last person to care really about the morality of abortion. I cast my lot with you years ago. We are what we are at this point in life. Still, you have to wonder sometimes. What would a baby choose, if it had the option of a challenging life or no life at all? Haven't you ever thought about it?"

"No. I really haven't. What's more, I won't think about it. My work stands for itself. No one can prove that I did anything wrong. Who can judge me? No one on this earth. That's for sure."

The longtime married couple sat silently, looking out the windows. The deer moved stealthily away into the forest.

Knowing that the truth would frighten her, Dr. Heller had been keeping things from his wife. His spells came with certain sensations in his brain and in his chest. His end felt near. Being the town's only abortionist exacted a toll, so many lies and compromises. Who had a right to judge him? If all the moralists would be honest, most abortions amount to a mercy killing. Society runs smoother with fewer welfare babies. He felt sure of that. Maybe Margaret Sanger and Planned Parenthood had that part right from the beginning. So much work left for Dr. Heller and so many obstacles. How would he get it all done?

18

Marcella knocked at the heavy glass-and-oak front door. No response. She tried to ring the doorbell, but heard nothing from the other side. It seemed odd that Ashley would invite her over to study, but not answer the door. Lights glowed out from the second-floor windows.

After knocking again, she decided to try the latch. Surprisingly, the door pushed open. "Hello, it's Marcella!" she hollered. No response. "Ashley, are you here?" Still nothing.

Another girl probably would have left well enough alone, but not Marcella. After the ten-minute walk to Ashley's house, she was in no mood to trudge back home without seeing her best friend. Maybe Ashley's mom took her to the store to buy some snacks. It wouldn't hurt to have a seat in the living room for five or ten minutes until they got back. Hopefully, they would buy Salt and Pepper potato chips. Next to coconut macaroons, chips tasted best for homework snacking.

After a few minutes of sitting quietly on the couch, Marcella thought she heard a sound upstairs. If her memory served, it was coming from Ashley's room. Perhaps her friend was home after all and hadn't heard Marcella knock.

The Featherstone family stood on ceremony a bit more than Marcella and her large, informal clan. While she knew barging in on Mrs. Featherstone would be a no-no, she felt sure that Ashley wouldn't bat an eye if Marcella went upstairs. They needed to get busy studying anyway.

Marcella cautiously climbed the stairs to the bedrooms above. Feeling like a top-secret spy, she put one foot in front of the other. As she got about halfway up, more muffled sounds seemed to be coming from Ashley's bedroom. One gentle step after another, she reached the top of the landing. To avoid an awkward situation, she planned to listen for the right moment and then knock on Ashley's door. Just as Marcella reached Ashley's room, the door behind her opened suddenly and someone let out a blood-curdling scream.

Marcella started screaming too. When she composed herself, she realized that the person behind her was Mrs. Featherstone. With the racket made by the screaming, Ashley's door opened.

Mrs. Featherstone, wearing a bathrobe and a towel around her head, asked nonchalantly, "What's going on out here?"

"Oh hi, Mrs. Featherstone. I'm just here for a study date with Ashley."

"Hello Marcella," Mrs. Featherstone said with a formal air to her voice. "I wasn't expecting you." The inference rang through loudly. One doesn't drop in on the Featherstone's unannounced.

Ashley grabbed Marcella's arm and pulled her into her room. Without pause for breathing she said, "Come on in, Marcella, we have a lot to cover. Mom, can you bring up some cookies. I think Marcella likes the macaroons."

"Sure, Ashley," Mrs. Featherstone said. "I will get you girls some milk too."

Everything about Ashley's room fascinated Marcella. Just having a room that she didn't share with her sister would be great. The fancy drapes in a damask pattern would just be gravy. Marcella stared at the large window with a Juliet balcony, imagining what it would be like to wake up each day and greet her subjects from the wrought iron railing. No wonder Ashley felt like a princess, and Marcella felt like a court jester.

"Your room never ceases to amaze me," Marcella gushed. "How do you stand living in the lap of luxury every day?"

"Yeah. It's nice I suppose. I'm here every day, so the fascination wears off. Believe me. Dad's out of town on business half the time. Mom is preoccupied with her social circle. Her Eastern Star group seems goofy to me, a crazy time-consuming hobby and so much work. She spends hours planning and attending events that would bore me to tears."

"Well, excuse your little Latina friend from the barrio while I ooh and ah at your room and your life for a minute. Your mom is so refined and dignified. Now, I love my family dearly, but just once to walk into a store with someone who didn't thoroughly embarrass me would be amazing. You haven't clothes shopped until your mom tries to negotiate down the price off the clearance rack. Such is life in the barrio."

"You live ten minutes away on Monticello Avenue. I am

pretty sure that Springfield doesn't even have a barrio. We don't have a Beverly Hills neighborhood either."

Marcella dramatically demonstrated her catwalk gait to Ashley's walk-in closet and threw open both doors. With as much melodrama as she could muster, she said "Compared with your closet, my room is a barrio. Your house is Beverly Hills." For emphasis, she grabbed an expensive handbag from one of the built-in, lighted shelves. After donning a hat, she strutted back and forth across the bedroom floor, modeling the purse.

"You are too much. Let's get busy studying. Chemistry is not my favorite subject and that test is coming tomorrow ready or not."

"Okay. We'll crack the books my studious friend. But first, how are you doing, kid?"

"I'm fine," Ashley said automatically. After thinking a moment, "Not really. I'm scared, confused, angry, and conflicted. I haven't got up the courage to tell Mom. I don't really want to tell anyone. The truth be told, I'm sorry I told Terrell. My best play would have been to figure it out myself and tell no one."

"It's a lot to handle alone. Fortunately, you have a super friend like yours truly who performs well in any crisis."

Ashley looked at Marcella and said, "Oh yeah, you stayed really cool during the last lab quiz when you tried to light the Bunsen burner with the gas control wide open. They probably heard you scream all the way to the cafeteria."

"The flame almost went up to the ceiling. Test Tube Terry did that on purpose."

"Yes," Ashley said. "It's called a lab quiz to see if we follow appropriate procedures before lighting a Bunsen burner. A little respect, it's Mr. Terry McEwen to us students. If you plan to create life-threatening situations in the lab, the instructor may need to rein you in a little. Maybe you should watch a few YouTube videos. Repeat after me, I am a strong and capable woman. Chemistry is easy for me."

Marcella burst out laughing. "You and those affirmations. Those words sound so not-like-me. Ashley Featherstone, are you hypnotizing me with your positive sayings? Next thing I know, you will be selling me Tupperware against my will."

Responding to the hurt look on Ashley's face, Marcella walked closer and patted her friend's shoulder. "You know what I mean. Of course, you are strong and capable, but you are also in high school. Those mantras sound stiff and not like the real you. I'd trust you to do anything, but you need to be yourself. Ask the inner you, what would super Ashley do?"

At that moment, Mrs. Featherstone arrived at the door with a plate of macaroons and two tumblers of milk. "Do about what?" she asked.

"Oh nothing, mom," Ashley said. "Crazy Marcella is always posing these hypotheticals."

"Yeah, crazy me and my far-out hypotheticals," Marcella repeated, scowling at Ashley while having her back to Mrs. Featherstone. "Thanks for the cookies, Mrs. Featherstone. These are my favorites! Sorry for startling you earlier."

"No problem. You're welcome." Mrs. Featherstone exited, leaving the door open.

"We better hit the books," Ashley said. "Did you bring your notes for chemistry class?"

"No," Marcella replied. "Yours are better anyways."

"Let's start memorizing those bromides."

"Too bad Terrell's not here," Marcella said. "He's good for a bromide now and then."

Ashley ignored the comment. Instead, she asked, "What

do you think happens to babies that never get born?"

"Um.... good question," Marcella said. "I haven't given it a ton of thought. Maybe God puts them back into the hopper, and they get born to someone else."

"We should ask Mrs. Warren. She studies up on this kind of thing. I think it's valuable information. You know, if either of us ever needs such information to make a decision."

Marcella could see the wheels turning in Ashley's head, which is just the reaction she hoped her visit might inspire.

19

"Let's go, T! You're our man! Won't you give us all you can?" Ashley and the other cheerleaders bounced up and down with each syllable. Their winter uniforms, white shirts, black skirts, and black-and-red vests, looked neat and crisp from a distance.

Sarah Warren sat alone, roughly halfway up the bleachers of the school gym. She smiled down at the cheerleaders as they waved their pompoms toward the half-full home seating area.

"Hey, Madison? Over here!" Sarah called out above the cheers and other pre-match noise.

Madison looked up and spotted the familiar face of the clinic protestor.

"Sarah, how are you?" Madison asked while sitting down uncomfortably close to someone she barely knew. Sarah Warren looked a little paunchier than Madison remembered. Maybe her casual clothes did less to hide the bulges. Madison obsessed over her own figure and sometimes the figure of other women as well. She'd have to give that some thought later.

"We meant to have coffee," Sarah said. "Where does the time go? What are you doing here?"

"My husband is the coach. He loves wrestling."

"Oh my gosh. That's so nice of you to come and support him. Make yourself comfortable. Tell me about your family. Do you and the coach have children?"

Madison unbuttoned her coat. Looking down she didn't see Zane or the wrestlers yet.

"Yes, we have two children. My husband's name is Zane, by the way. My little girl, Shelby, is four going on fourteen. She is a spitfire and takes after me. My mom prayed her down on me, a little girl just like the one that tormented her. Braden just turned 18 months. He's quiet and smiles a lot. Those kids make our lives amazing every day. My mom babysits while I work … and when I sneak out to the occasional wrestling meet. Truthfully, this is my first one this year. Do you have family here in town?"

"No husband. Charles passed away many years ago. We didn't have children. My parents are still living, near Chicago. Most of my brothers and sisters live up that way too. With five siblings, I wasn't under too much pressure to produce children. My sisters did that for my parents. My freelance accounting business pays the bills. It will be ten years next June since I went out on my own. The small business, entrepreneur life is perfect for me—so much freedom. Accounting can be a bit monotonous and lonely, but it frees me up to pursue other passions. Walks and trips to Starbucks get me out of the condo."

"And an occasional protest," Madison said smiling. "You can protest in the morning and audit someone's books in the afternoon."

"Oh, that's funny," Sarah said. "That needs to be on my business card. Actually, I only have time to protest on Mondays. Too much work and other commitments fill up the rest of the time. How long have you been with the clinic?"

"Well, that's an interesting subject. I plan to give my notice on Monday. Planned Parenthood will have to get along without me in a couple of weeks."

"Oh great, I think. Why are you moving on? Did you find something better?"

"I'm sure you'd love to hear that it had something to do with the folks praying and protesting out front, but not so much. My aim always was to love and care for women at a vulnerable place in their lives, but I didn't see Planned Parenthood as a permanent job. When I started working at the clinic, I believed we were providing quality health care services. Now, I'm not sure anyone is healthier after visiting our clinic. The mother ends up mentally scarred and sometimes physically as well. The child ends up dead. As for the staff, the whole thing gets to us too. The people yelling out front gets tiresome."

Sarah stared at Madison, making her feel uncomfortable. Could the older woman see the hurt and disappointment? "I think you are a brave young woman. You tried to help others in one way, and now you are moving on based on your experience. Nothing wrong with learning and growing."

Madison held back tears. Though she barely knew Sarah, any port in a storm looked good at this moment. She reached over and held Sarah's hand.

"I feel guilty," Madison said. "After counseling women to have abortions, now I'm not sure how I feel about the procedure anymore." Tears flowed.

A wrestling mom across the aisle gave Madison a concerned look. She released her grip on Sarah's hand and pulled away.

"Oh honey, Jesus understands," Sarah said in a hushed tone. "We've all made a million mistakes. Talk to Him about how you feel. Quitting your job shows you have integrity. Your conscience will guide you right, if you let Him."

Madison pulled a wad of clean tissues from her purse. Sarah dabbed her mascara and blew her nose.

After a loud buzzer sounded, the announcer welcomed everyone and introduced the home wrestling team. Terrell led his teammates onto the mats, and Zane walked out of the locker room behind them. The boys fist bumped one another as each of the starters were introduced, forming a growing semi-circle. When the last wrestler joined them, they all jogged over to Coach Zane and shouted something unintelligible. Then the visiting team responded to their own intros in a similar manner.

As the first match began, Madison changed the subject, explaining a few of the finer points of scoring. She interpreted the official's hand signals and taught Sarah a little about the weight classes.

"So, that makes it fair," Madison explained. "Each wrestler competes against someone in the same weight class."

"You know a lot about wrestling," Sarah said smiling.

"My husband *is* the coach," Madison responded with pride. "I'd look like a goof if I didn't know a few of the basics. Which brings up a question for you. What attracts you to this macho contest of brute strength and agility?"

"Oh, I teach Sunday school at Springfield Community

Fellowship. One of the wrestlers and a couple of the cheer-leaders are students in my class. See that girl down there with the blonde hair, that's Ashley." Sarah pointed to make sure Madison could identify the right girl.

Madison's mind froze as her two worlds collided. As if she didn't feel emotional enough, now this almost stranger pointed directly at her client. The girl from the health center stood cheering, not thirty feet from where they sat. Madison reminded herself that Sarah didn't know anything about her counseling of Ashley.

"The one cheering next to her is Wanda," Sarah continued. "I promised them at the beginning of the school year that I would make it to one of their games. This is my first wrestling match or meet or game—what do you call it?"

Both women chuckled. "I'm so glad you came. It's a wrestling meet. Zane is aware I plan to give my notice at the clinic, but he's preoccupied with the team right now. He needs to turn the program around fast. Coaches don't get these opportunities very often. He just adores wrestling and mentoring the kids. I'm sure it's great for the boys to have him as a role model. He's the most level-headed person I know. Thank you for inviting me over to sit with you. It's nice to make a new friend."

"Call me anytime. Let me write down my number on a piece of paper." As Sarah reached in her purse for a notepad and pen, she asked, "Where are you going to church these days?"

"Bad question," Madison noted as both women chuckled. "Since I left college, I've only been to church a handful of times. Usually, it's when we visit Zane's family around Christmas."

"What keeps you away?"

"I'm not sure," Madison said. "Guilt maybe. Zane and I drifted away from church when we started dating. Now, life seems so busy all the time. We cherish our Sundays together."

"Well, he's allowed to come to church with you. Bring the kids. Free babysitting for an hour or two. How about meeting me next Sunday at 10:30 a.m.?"

Madison thought for a few minutes. "I can talk it over with him," Madison said. "No promises, but we may show up one of these Sundays and surprise you."

The announcer read Terrell's name over the loudspeaker.

"Oh, that boy is in my class too. He doesn't come to Sunday School quite as often. He's dating Ashley, I think."

Madison nearly swallowed the stick of gum she had been chewing. Her violent coughing drew the gaze of Ashley and a couple of the other cheerleaders. Recognition flooded Ashley's face before she turned pale. Moments later, Ashley sprinted toward a side door as Madison's eyes followed her.

"That's a little odd," Sarah said. "I wonder why Ashley left so abruptly?"

"Teenagers," Madison said while collecting her purse and coat. "I hate to cry and run, but I forgot something I left on at home." With that, she hustled down the steps and out toward the parking lot.

Madison exited the building just in time to see Ashley climb into her Mustang. She hurried in that direction. When she arrived at the car, Ashley sat crying in the front seat. Knocking on the window drew an unexpected response. Ashley motioned her away with a wave of her right hand, but Madison wouldn't leave.

"Ashley, I just have to tell you something." After thinking it over for a minute or so, the girl lowered the driver's side window with the push of a button. "You need to know that I would never tell anyone what we talked about. I've barely met Sarah Warren. It's a small-town. Everyone bumps into everyone eventually, but trust me. Your case is confidential with me. If you want to talk again sometime, I will be working at the clinic only two more weeks. But I'd be glad to give you my personal cell phone number if you want it?"

The young lady shook her head no and rolled up the window. Madison walked slowly to her car feeling defeated.

20

"Zane, I'm glad you're home. I heated up some veal parm for you. Come sit at the island when you are ready," Madison said.

"Will do. Let me change into my sweat pants and wash my hands."

In a few minutes, Zane appeared in the kitchen and passionately kissed Madison on the lips. "Why are the kids in bed so early? Not that I'm complaining?"

"Mom offered to keep them, so they are over at her house. Braden missed his nap and went down for the night. The little princess played herself ragged with Mom. She had an imaginary tea party, baked cupcakes, put together some puzzles, made milkshakes, etc. Typical Shelby-thon at Grandma's house. Mom got her in bed early too. It looks like you and I can have an evening by ourselves."

"That sounds scrumptious, like this veal," Zane said as he sat down to eat.

"Did you guys win your meet?"

"We did," Zane said. "I thought I saw you before it started."

The veal practically disappeared as Zane ravenously devoured each bite. Madison refilled his water glass at one point. "Do you think we should find a church around here?" she asked.

"Um, I haven't thought much about it," Zane said. "We are both kind of busy, but maybe. If you are going to be off work a while, the fellowship might be nice for you. Our parents would be thrilled to know the kids are in Sunday School. It's probably a good idea to expose them to faith. I have fond memories of church school."

"Maybe I could check online. Let's give it some thought and visit around a bit. No sense jumping in without seeing the options."

Zane nodded yes as his phone buzzed. He swallowed the last bite of food in his mouth. "Yes, this is Coach Matthews." After a pause, "Oh, I understand. Let me check around and see if anyone else from the team knows where he went. It may be a few minutes, but we'll find him. Call me back if Terrell shows up at home."

Zane hung up his phone and stared at the screen.

"Is Terrell missing?" Madison asked.

"He didn't make it home. His mother is worried because he usually calls unless he's working at his part-time job or at wrestling. I suppose he left school after the meet when everyone else took off. He should have been home half an hour ago. Not sure what's going on."

"I think I saw him on my way back from Mom's house.

He turned into the park off Redding Street. Whoever I saw wore a letter jacket from your high school and looked like a wrestler from the back. It seemed weird to me because everyone is avoiding the running trails now with a killer on the loose."

"Teenage boys don't necessarily view danger like everyone else," Zane said. "Superman syndrome ... they feel invincible. I know I did. Let me call a couple of his friends from the team first. He's probably playing video games at someone's house."

Zane called Scott, Tim and two other wrestlers. No one had heard from Terrell since the meet ended. After gulping down pudding for dessert, Zane grabbed his keys.

"Maybe we should take a ride by the park, and you can show me where you think you saw him enter."

"Okay, if you think it's safe. What if Terrell is fine and sitting at his girlfriend's house, but you and I get murdered looking for him?"

"Honey," Zane said defensively. "Do you think I would let a psycho killer harm my sweetheart? Besides, I have a golf club in the back of the truck. I can hit the killer upside of the head with my five iron." He smiled and tugged on Madison's sleeve to position her for a kiss.

As she got her coat and purse, Zane peeled and wolfed down an orange that was sitting on the counter. The pair jumped in his pick-up. The short drive over to the trailhead took less than ten minutes. As Zane turned off the engine and grabbed his phone from the cupholder, Madison noticed that the street looked deserted.

Madison's eyes quickly adjusted to the dim lighting cast by a single streetlight reflecting off the snow. As they crossed Redding Avenue and took a few steps onto the bike trail, Madison switched on the flashlight app from her phone. Zane stepped on a twig, snapping it. Madison tried to stifle a squeal, but the noise sent a rabbit hopping into the woods.

"Settle down, sweetie. I stepped on a piece of wood. You are going to give me a heart attack if you scream every few steps."

Madison wrapped her arm around Zane's and walked in lockstep with him. If a murderer lurked in the shadows, he would have to take them both out. After fifty feet or so, Zane slowed and stopped. He signaled Madison to remain silent as he listened. The forested area yielded only the sound of rustling leaves. Madison shined her light in that direction. A suspicious-looking racoon stared back at them with masked eyes and a felonious look on its face.

They continued walking down the path another hundred feet until Zane again motioned for her to stop. "Shine the phone light over in that direction," Zane said pointing to the left of the trail.

Madison did as instructed. The snowy grass lay flat as if something or someone had been dragged from the pathway. Peering down the short embankment, they saw nothing unusual at first.

"Let me borrow your phone," Zane whispered. "Stay here."

Madison wanted to protest, but she handed him the phone and looked anxiously up and down the trail. Zane carefully descended the embankment four or five feet. He lost his footing in the snow-covered grass and stumbled without falling.

"You alright?" Madison asked.

"Yes, I see something," he said.

Just then a gust of wind blew Madison's hair a little and she stifled a scream. It felt like an icy hand on the back of her neck.

"Oh no. Oh no. It's Terrell."

Zane pointed the phone flashlight at a crumpled mass near some underbrush. He knelt down to check on him. Moments later, he stood and hurried up the embankment. With the bright light of the flashlight app, Madison could see a swipe of dark red blood on the palm of Zane's hand.

"Call 911," he said, handing her the phone.

21

An hour later, Madison was sitting across from two detectives in a conference room at the police station. The larger of the two men needed his eyebrows trimmed in the worst way. Madison wished she had her husband's electric trimmer. His overall appearance wasn't too bad, salt and pepper hair, large shoulders, and beefy arms, but those eyebrows made her skin crawl. Eventually, he spoke.

"I'm Detective Lawson and this is Detective English. We want to ask you a few questions about how you and your husband found the body."

"I understand," Madison replied, nodding her head and trying not to stare at the man's exuberant eyebrows.

"We understand you and Zane were actually out looking

for the boy when you found his body," English said. "Is that right?"

She stared attentively at the blonde man who appeared younger than Lawson. His face bore scars from years of acne, but his eyes shone clear blue and youthful.

"Yes, Terrell is a wrestler on the high school team that Zane coaches. My husband arrived home after a meet and was eating supper. Terrell's mother called and asked if Zane knew why her son hadn't made it home yet."

"I see." Lawson glanced at his notes. "How did you or your husband know where to look?"

Madison jumped in. "On my way home from the meet, I thought I might have seen Terrell jogging. Not knowing for sure if it was him, I wondered why anyone would be jogging at night through the park in light of the recent murders. When Terrell's mother called, Zane and I began our search at the park, near where I thought I saw him go in. We planned to follow the path and come out the other side which is near Terrell's house."

Det. Lawson asked, "How did you discover the body? It was pretty dark out, even with snow covering the ground."

"We used my cell phone. It has a flashlight app that puts out quite a bit of light." Madison tapped her foot nervously.

"Did you see Terrell's body first or was it your husband?" Detective English asked.

"First, Zane saw a change in the snow near the trail," Madison explained. "It looked like something may have fallen or been dragged off into the brush." Thinking about Terrell, Madison could hear her voice crack at the end of her last sentence. She wanted to stop and cry over the young man: a life so young snuffed out.

"So, did you stand on the trail and look into the woods?' Det. English asked.

"I did, but Zane borrowed my phone and descended down the small embankment. He didn't see anything at first, but soon spotted Terrell's body over by some bushes. Zane checked to see if he might still be alive."

"Did your husband try to render aid to the young man?" Lawson asked.

"Yes. He knelt down and felt for a pulse. When he did, it was clear to him that Terrell was deceased. Zane got a little blood on his hand, and honestly, I think that freaked him out. He ran back to where I stood and told me to call 911."

The questioning went on a little while longer, but the two men seemed satisfied with her version of events. They thanked her, and Detective Lawson showed her out of the conference room to a waiting area.

"Thank you again, Mrs. Matthews. We still need to question your husband. If you want, you can retrieve your purse from the receptionist and head on home. Myself or someone else can drop off Mr. Matthews when we're done."

"Can I just wait for him and drive him?"

"If you want to wait for him, it might take a couple of hours or more. We have to type up the notes from your interview before we can start with him. A patrol officer will take you home. Just as a precaution, we are looking over your husband's truck. That could take a couple of days."

"It's getting late. Could you interview him in the morning?" Madison asked. She pleaded with her eyes, even though it required looking at those eyebrows for an extended time.

"I'm sorry," Lawson said. "We want to get the information while it's fresh in everyone's mind. Also, a killer is on the loose. The sooner we can get all the facts, the sooner we can get him off the streets."

"I understand," Madison said, feeling dejected.

She collected her purse and a uniformed officer escorted her out of the building. When she got home, the lights she and Zane had left on welcomed her. After phoning her mother with an update, she put a pod in the Keurig. Soon she was hugging a large mugful of warmth. Although she didn't plan to watch anything in particular, the television provided background noise in the all-too-quiet house. How often had she wished for a few minutes of peace and silence? Her vision didn't include detectives grilling her husband down at police headquarters after she and Zane discovered a dead teenager in the park.

The couch felt extra comfortable after sitting on the hard chair at the police station. Madison picked up her Kindle and thumbed through a novel she'd long intended to read. One more swallow of coffee warmed her. Draped in the warm, chocolate-brown cashmere blanket, her eyes become very heavy.

Hours later, she woke, hearing Zane's key in the front door.

Madge sat behind her desk, shuffling a stack of papers as Madison entered.

"Hello, Ms. Abzug. May I have a few moments?"

"Certainly, Madison," Madge croaked while reaching for her coffee cup. "How did things go on Saturday?"

Madison noticed bruising on one side of Madge's face. She tried not to stare. A newspaper laid neatly folded on her desk. Pictures of the dead young women and Terrell peered up at Madison making her feel uncomfortable. Her boss's voice sounded even lower and more gravelly than normal. "How is your mouth doing?" Madison asked. "Do you feel better today?"

"The swelling isn't too bad, but I'm not on solid food

yet. Thanks to Oxycodone and that Quaker Oats guy for getting me through this morning. Sweet of you to ask, doll. Now, back to you. What happened on Saturday?"

"Well, that's why I need to speak with you. Seeing a procedure in person became quite an eye-opener."

"In what way?"

Madison shifted in her seat and tucked a wisp of hair behind her ear. "Up until now, my only knowledge of abortions came second-hand. It seemed clinical, neat, and sterile from a distance. In person, it's a whole other animal. All the blood and gore. Worse yet, Dr. Heller and Natasha joked around so callously."

"I hope old Doc Heller wasn't too crass. He gets a bit graphic in his descriptions. You have to understand though, he's been doing this for many years."

"He said inappropriate things. They were disrespectful to the client while she was under anesthesia. That's really not the heart of the matter. I understood that the baby, I mean the fetus, couldn't feel anything, but this little one pulled away from the instruments. It could sense danger or feel pain or something. I don't know. It shocked me and aroused my maternal instincts in a primal way."

Madge adjusted her huge glasses as if to get a better look at Madison. "Dear one, you are getting confused. I can see it on your face. Look, life is messy. Abortions involve blood, like most surgical procedures. We are doing the best thing to help these young women. Whether you stay or go, the clinic will keep doing procedures and keep helping women with their health issues. Don't you want to be part of the solution? Your attitude and personality are so well suited to this work. You make sure women get the best care."

Madison thought for a few moments. Until now, she hadn't known how to express what she felt. Madge always seemed to get the upper hand and overpower her emotionally. Madison seldom even tried to argue with her, but not this time. She determined to speak her mind and stand up for herself.

"Ms. Abzug, I appreciate all that you've done for me. I really do. You've been a mentor, and your opinion means a lot to me. I respect you so much. But this job just isn't right for me at this point in my life. I have to give my two weeks' notice."

"Your mind is made up?" Madge asked with smug intonation and a shoulder shrug. Madison nodded her head. "Well, that's truly unfortunate. You have a real gift for working with women. If you change your mind in the next few days, let me know. Nothing is irrevocable until you walk out the door on your last day. We run such a small office here; we're just one person deep at each position. I'll have to start hunting for a replacement right away."

"I understand," Madison said. "Don't worry. There is no chance that I will change my mind."

Back in her office, Madison began shaking. She wasn't quite sure why. Standing up to Madge felt empowering, but also draining. Just as she didn't know what to expect on her first day at the Center, leaving gave her a rush of excitement. None of this made sense in her mind, but her heart told her she was doing the right thing.

Without knocking, Vanessa entered and slid into the chair opposite Madison.

"Your 9:30 is here, but I want to ask you something first. Did I hear you giving Madge your two-week notice?"

"Yes, Miss Nosey-Pants," Madison said. "The walls in this place must be paper thin."

"Actually, I was listening through the intercom," Vanessa said, a sheepish look crossing her face.

"You are something, girl. Honestly, I just need to move

on, but I will miss working with you and even Madge to a lesser degree."

Madison stood up and walked around the desk. Hugging Vanessa a few seconds longer than usual, the loss of another relationship tugged at her heart. By now, she knew what leaving a job meant. Although everyone talks about staying in touch, everything changes when you no longer see friends on a daily basis. The word goodbye never sounded good to Madison.

Vanessa exited and soon returned, ushering in a brunette. Without looking at her file, Madison guessed that the woman must be at least age 30. Madison shook her hand.

"I'm Martina."

For the first time in a long while, Madison stayed on her own side of the desk to speak with a client. She eyed the woman's crisp pants suit and neatly cut hair. Simple white gold earrings matched a thin necklace which supported a multi-faceted amethyst. This redhead looked sharp, pulled together.

"Hi, I'm Madison. What brings you in today?" She hated it when she hadn't had time to read the client's folder prior to an interview. In this case, she'd been tied up with Madge.

"The short version is that I want an abortion as soon as possible," Martina said.

"Okay, that's what they do here." The word 'they' surprised Madison. Did she really feel so removed from the Planned Parenthood mission already? "How did you come to this conclusion?"

"I get that you have a job to do, counseling and all, but I need to get back to work. So, let's make this as quick as possible. I've been married for three years. My husband is a lying piece of animal dung, and he's fooling around on me. We both pretend he isn't, but his phone messages and texts say otherwise. The last thing I want is another child if we are getting a divorce."

Although unusual for a woman to be this sure, Madison had seen other clients that needed little convincing. Something about Martina's resolve didn't sit well with Madison. Maybe it involved her own baggage from last Saturday, but she couldn't be sure. Caution signs appeared in Madison's brain and she tried to slow Martina down.

"Please don't get me wrong," Madison said. "It's completely your choice about the abortion, but I'd like to go through a few questions that we use to help people determine which procedure is right for them."

"Look, I know what's right for me. I'm telling you that I want a physical abortion. I tried the chemical thing before and it nearly put me under. The sooner I can get this thing out of my body, the better. First available appointment is probably good for me—the sooner the better. Can we just get on with the required paperwork and skip the hoopla?"

Madison stared at Martina and thought about the unfortunate life growing within her. For the first time since she worked at the clinic, Madison felt gut-wrenching sorrow for the unborn child.

"Sure. Let me get you a package that you can fill out. Do you have insurance?"

"Yes. What will the co-pay be? I want the cheapest option."

"Possibly, there could be some financial assistance, depending on your income level. The financial aid form is included in this folder. Would you like to fill out the forms here or take them with you? You can drop them off later today or tomorrow, if you like. That won't stop us from making an appointment for your procedure. We have openings this Saturday. Can you do 11 a.m. or would you prefer 1 p.m.?"

"I think 1 p.m. would work best for me. My boy has a dental appointment on Saturday morning."

Madison stood up and handed the packet of forms to Martina. "Very good. You are scheduled for 1 p.m. Saturday. Get the paperwork back to us tomorrow if possible."

"Thank you. I will drop off the papers tomorrow at lunchtime."

23

Nearly a week passed with no news about the investigation of Terrell's murder. Madison began to wonder about the competency of the local police detectives. After all, murder ranked as the rarest of crimes in Springfield. Except for a couple of passion-related spousal murders, there hadn't been a similar crime mentioned on the news for as long as Zane had been teaching at the high school.

"Shelby, do you want to go to the playground by Grandma's house today?"

"Yes, Mommy. That would be great, great, great!" Shelby bounced up and down as she answered.

Zane entered the family room, dressed in warm-up pants and a forest-green Henley shirt. After smooching

Madison, he picked up Braden from his spot on the couch. Sitting down next to Madison, he jiggled Braden on his knee and looked at Shelby. "Shel, what if I finish up with wrestling practice early and meet you and Mommy at the playground?"

"That would be great, Daddy!"

"You haven't heard anything from the detective, have you?" Madison asked.

"No, babe. You know I'd tell you if he called or anything."

"Why would anyone kill a young man like that?" Madison tilted her head to the side as she finished her question. "It doesn't fit with the other cases, women in their thirties."

"That's a good question. I guess the police only suspected me for about five minutes because they just have no clue. Since all three victims had dealings with your clinic, they think there could be a connection. The perpetrator could have ties through one of the victims or someone who had a procedure long ago. I wonder if it's an angry boyfriend."

"They asked me questions about the demonstrators," Madison said. "They seemed to be hypothesizing about the killer being a religious nut who would kill people involved in abortions. However, if it were someone trying to stop the clinic, you would think they would have targeted the abortion doctor or staff, not patients."

"Glad you are quitting there, by the way," Zane said. "I didn't say much when you told me because I didn't want to sound preachy. You already know I had reservations about that job."

"I know. Leaving feels good. Don't get me wrong. In some ways, it feels like abandoning them when they need me most. Maybe my going away present could be solving the murders so Madge and Vanessa can relax. What do you think, Dr. Watson? Can we track down the killer in a week?"

Zane reached over and pulled Madison close. "We can give it some thought and prayer. Did the two women have anything in common other than visiting the clinic? Did either of them have an angry or deranged husband? Was there a super religious parent in the picture? I think your mom could kill an abortion doctor or two."

"Stop joking around. Mom's weapons are spiritual, not made by Smith and Wesson. You know what's weird? Neither of the murdered women, nor Terrell's girlfriend, went through with their abortions. They all cancelled."

"Maybe that's the connection!" Zane exclaimed.

Braden clapped his hands in reaction to Daddy's excited voice.

"It's possible. Ashley and Terrell canceled in front of Dr. Heller. Could he be mad enough about a cancellation to kill someone? You would have to be mentally ill to commit murder over a missed appointment. It also doesn't make sense for business. A lot of the women who cancel once or twice eventually come back later and have their procedure anyway."

"Maybe it wasn't cancellations, but some other aspect of planning to get an abortion. I wonder if the murderer could be a pro-life protestor? Suppose the killer didn't know the procedures were cancelled. What if one of the protestors just took down license numbers on abortion day and traced them back to specific clients through their plates?"

Madison thought about Zane's theory. It made her shudder to think a strangler may have been standing on the other side of that fence as she arrived for work. Madison wasn't convinced that any of their theories were even close to correct, but she had a plan to find out more.

24

Zane and the entire wrestling team filed into the back of the church. Together in single file, Terrell's closest friends and teammates walked to the front and filed by the closed casket. Due to the gruesome manner of strangulation with a wire, Terrell's parents didn't want others to see his body.

In the front row, Terrell's mother and father sat with his sister, acknowledging each one who stopped to offer condolences. Ashley sat sobbing a few rows back with her mother. When his turn came to pause at the casket, Zane offered a silent prayer with his head bowed. As he turned toward the family, Terrell's parents refused to look at him. Even so, he walked to where they were sitting and said only two words. "Deepest sympathy."

On the way to his seat, Zane noticed Ashley and nodded to her. Then, he sat with his wrestlers in the second-to-last row. The service went by quickly. Most of the songs and words didn't register with the coach. However, Terrell's teammate, Scott, offered a moving eulogy, and Zane hung on every word. He felt great pride in Scott's ability to rise to the occasion.

Mostly, Zane spent the funeral service thinking about the first time he met Terrell. As a freshman, the scrawny black kid strutted into practice like he owned the place. He barely looked winded after the conditioning part of practice. Other guys sucked wind, and two of them even tossed their cookies. When Zane taught the freshmen the most basic wrestling holds, Terrell impressed by his commitment to getting his positioning exactly right. The attention to detail showed Zane that Terrell might be something special. Three months later, Terrell won a spot in the district tournament—one of only four freshmen to accomplish it.

As the service ended, everyone moved to their cars to join the processional to the cemetery. Zane and the wrestlers rode in one of the high school's minibuses, the quietest ride Zane had ever taken with a bunch of teenagers.

At the cemetery, Detective Lawson stared at Zane, sending a message that he wasn't beyond suspicion at this point. This worried Zane, not that they would try to convict the wrong man. If they focused on him, the police might not be following up on other leads. If they put their resources into tracking the one person he knew didn't kill Terrell, how would they catch the real killer?

25

Madison put Shelby and Braden down for the night about eight p.m. She didn't expect Zane to call for another couple of hours. Four of his wrestlers made it into the state tournament. The two-day event meant that wrestlers would stay overnight in the capital city with Coach Zane as their chaperone. It meant little sleep, making sure his charges didn't get any bright ideas in the middle of the night.

About halfway through a novel, Madison settled onto the couch with a hot chocolate nearby. The first hour passed uneventfully. As the action in the book picked up, she turned the pages faster and faster. Around nine thirty, Madison bolted upright when she heard the distinctive sound of glass breaking toward the back of the house. Home alone with the kids, many things went through her mind. With no way to explain away the sound, she looked around the living room for a weapon.

Madison scrambled to the fireplace and grabbed the heavy steel poker. Like a half-crazed bear protecting her cubs, she hustled to the kitchen with weapon in hand. A very scared-looking Shelby whimpered when she saw her wild-eyed mother.

"Oh Shelby! What are you doing out of bed?"

Shelby's lower lip puckered and tears formed at the corners of her little eyes. "I sorry, Mommy. I wanted a drink of juice."

With glass everywhere and no shoes on herself, the only option was to retrieve the broom from the closet in the pantry. "Don't move a muscle. Let mommy get the broom and sweep up the mess. I'm afraid you are going to get glass in your feet. Stay right there."

Shelby began to cry harder.

After retrieving her own shoes and a broom, Madison swept up the glass from around her daughter's feet. Shelby obediently stood still until her mother deposited the last shard in a cardboard shoebox. Madison picked up Shelby and carried her into the living room – kissing her over and over. Wait here, and I will bring you some juice.

Retrieving a plastic cup, Madison poured apple juice to the halfway point. She heard Shelby talking in the other room, but could not make out what she was saying.

"I will be in there in just a minute, honey."

Shelby's voice trailed off. Madison carried the juice into the living room, but her daughter was nowhere to be found. It seemed odd that Shelby would go to bed without the juice that had just caused the near-catastrophe in the kitchen. Walking up the hallway toward Shelby's room,

Madison again heard her daughter talking—this time in a much quieter tone. Shivers went down her spine. She burst into the room.

"Shelby, who are you talking to?"

As she entered Shelby's room, she saw her daughter lying in bed, neatly tucked in. Madison handed her the cup of juice, and Shelby took a drink.

"Who were you talking to, honey?"

"Him." Shelby pointed behind Madison.

Madison screamed as she turned around. There stood Zane smiling sheepishly. "I'm home early. Our guys lost and we're out of the tournament, so we decided to head back early."

Her heart pounding out of her chest, Madison slapped Zane across bicep. "You scared me half to death."

"So sorry, hon." Zane took a few steps and hugged his wife until she stopped shaking. He smoothed her hair and kissed her on the cheek several times.

"I guess I'm a little jumpy," Madison said. "Shelby broke a glass in the kitchen. As I was cleaning it up, you must have come in through the garage."

"Daddy, kiss me too," Shelby said impatiently.

And he did.

26

Madison's last week at Planned Parenthood flew by. By Thursday, she'd booked only one abortion for Saturday. It wasn't out of any willful negligence, but few women called the clinic and no one walked in all week. Calling the list of prior contacts held little appeal, but she made her way through the first fifteen names on the, minus Ashley Featherstone. Knowing the circumstances with Terrell, the last thing that young woman needed was someone pressuring her about an abortion. None of the other fourteen women called back, and Madison felt fine with the lack of response. It surprised her how much her attitude about abortion had changed in just a couple of weeks.

"Hey, Madison. Are you ready for your lunch out with Madge and me?" Vanessa grinned as she juggled her handbag from one arm to another.

"Yep. Where are we going?"

"I told Madge that you liked the Tex-Mex place off Bechtel."

"Excellent!"

"Madge is meeting us, so let's head over there."

After the short ride to La Grande Fajita, Madison and Vanessa strode inside and looked around. Madge waived while peeking around the side of a pillar, blocking their view of the table where she was sitting. As they approached, Madison got a shock. Dr. Heller smiled from the chair next to Madge. He rose and bowed slightly to Vanessa and Madison.

"I hope you don't mind that I asked Dr. Heller to join us," Madge said.

"Not at all," Madison replied disingenuously.

"Thank you," Dr. Heller said. "I feel a little sheepish about the way I behaved the other day and hope to make amends. You've been such a good patient for several years, and I probably felt too comfortable around you. Madge and I talked, and she told me I may have offended you. Hopefully, my callous behavior didn't influence your decision to leave the clinic. If so, please reconsider."

Madison just stared with her mouth agape. Here was her gynecologist who she'd never seen outside his office until the day she helped him kill a baby. Now, he apparently felt remorse for inappropriate remarks. To atone, he was crashing her farewell lunch with Madge and Vanessa, but also paying the tab for it. She found it hard to get her head around the situation. Madison managed to respond after a lengthy and awkward silence. "No problem. My mind is made up though. It's time for a change."

Madge took the lead in turning the conversation toward ordering. The waiter arrived on cue with iced teas for each of the ladies and a beer for the doctor. After selecting fajitas, burritos, and extra guacamole, the conversation restarted.

"So, what new adventure lured you away from the clinic, Madison?" Dr. Heller asked.

"As you know, but my coworkers don't yet, I am pregnant with my third child."

"No way!" Vanessa nearly shouted.

"That's wonderful," Madge said. "Congratulations."

"This is number three for me. My mom has been great babysitting the other two for me, but watching three young children is a bit much to ask. I decided to stay home with my kids for at least a couple of years. This will allow me have one more year with Shelby before she trots off to kindergarten. Staying home is the right move for me right now."

"Good for you, honey," Vanessa said. "I had to work when my kids were little, and I always regretted it. Now, my little monsters are thrilled to have an hour after school by themselves before I get home."

After the foursome ordered, an awkward silence fell over the group. Madison munched chips and tried to avoid eye contact with Dr. Heller. This proved a mean trick as he was seated directly across from her, and his eyes seemed glued to her.

"Well, thank you all for allowing me to join you today," Dr. Heller finally said. "Madge and I have known each other for many years. Her work with the clinic does untold good for our community, and I feel honored to be part of it. Let's toast to Madge."

Madison tried to keep her mouth shut. She thought about Dr. Heller referring to a fetus as a little wiggler. It made her sick to her stomach, but she raised her glass anyway.

"You are a blessing, Dr. Heller," Madge said with exaggerated gravitas. "We simply could not have served Springfield all these years without a dedicated public servant physician such as yourself. I know you don't do it for the money. The little compensation you receive is not nearly worth the hassles and risks."

"Does this mean I won't be getting a check this month." Dr. Heller leaned back in his chair and laughed heartily at his own joke. Madge chuckled while Madison shot a glance over at Vanessa.

Madison doubted the altruism of Dr. Heller's service, though she imagined his willingness had more to do with sadism than compassion. She simply must find a new gynecologist to see her through this pregnancy.

"I remember when you first came to the clinic," Madge said. "We needed a replacement when Doc Blanchard was about to retire."

"I do indeed. Honestly, the extra income sounded good back then. New to town, I hadn't built up my gynecological practice yet. Four Saturdays a month helped pay for my Cynthia's braces in no time. Later, I began to see the importance of the clinic's mission."

Vanessa tried to change the subject, "Madison, I guess your mom will be glad that you are moving on from the clinic."

"Yes, I imagine so," Madison replied. "She had reservations from the start about me working there."

"Don't tell me she's one of those religious nuts?" Dr. Heller asked.

"Her faith is important to her. She feels that all children are a gift from God—even those who come into the world under difficult circumstances. When I started with the clinic, I focused on serving the women and making sure underprivileged women get the healthcare they deserve. Over time, I better understand my mother's views."

Dr. Heller cleared his throat and started turning a bit red. "There's a big difference between a small amount of tissue and a baby."

"I completely agree." Madge said. "Tissue is not a child. It's just part of a bodily function until a human life is born and breathing on its own. Women have a right to decide if they want to parent a child. Others have no say in the matter, not the state and certainly not the church."

"That's the whole premise behind Planned Parenthood, but I'm not so sure anymore," Madison said. "This thought occurred to me the other day. Why shouldn't the baby have a right choose? Why do we feel like the mother's opinion counts more than the child's right to live and make decisions for himself?"

"You are one mixed-up lady," Dr. Heller said.

"I'm sure Madison ..." Vanessa tried to jump in, but Dr. Heller was having none of it.

Seething with anger, he launched into a speech that Madison found quite condescending. "Look, raising a child is a lot more of an investment than having sex with a partner you may have only met once. It's insane to think that children are better off coming into the world with every disadvantage. Would you want to be raised by some crack addict mother who doesn't even want to be a parent? Can you imagine the added crime, poverty, and human suffering that would result if these women had no avenue to end unwanted pregnancy? Madge's clinic does more to end human suffering than any church or other institution in Springfield."

"I understand your point of view," Madison said. "First, we haven't had any crack addicts wander through since

I've been working at the clinic. Yes, some of the women are short on money, but most of them have other children. They figured out how to raise them. At one time, I shared your thoughts about tissue and fetuses, but my thoughts on the matter have evolved. Frankly, I don't see how you can look at an ultrasound of a little life and cut it up into parts like so much filet mignon." She said the last part to twist the knife a little.

Madison didn't mind discussing the matter further, but Dr. Heller's face looked like a tomato that could explode at any moment. His growing rage frightened Madison. Besides, he wasn't going to change his mind—not after all these years and all those dead fetuses.

When he composed himself just a bit, he pushed himself away from the table, got up, and left without a word.

27

Ashley's mother breezed into her room and opened the plantation shutters. Sun reflected off the snowy branches of the oak tree. She paused to watch her husband back the car out of their garage onto the quiet cul de sac. "Up and at'em, Sunshine. You are not spending one more day moping around the house. Your dad went to get us some donuts. He is under strict orders not to come back without the Boston crème confections that you love. After breakfast, you and I *are* going shopping."

Turning over, Ashley looked at her mother through bleary eyes. "I don't want to get up yet."

"Look honey, I know you are still hurting over Terrell. That's normal, but you can mourn him just as well down at the mall getting new shoes for winter. You've collected quite a collection of open-toed sandals and tennis shoes. We live in Ohio. Sandals won't work for the weather we have coming our way."

"I don't care about my feet," Ashley said. "Maybe my toes will freeze and fall off, and I won't have to go out ever again."

"Well, that's one melodramatic option, but as your mother, I have to nix that idea. One of my jobs is to get you and your feet safely into your twenties. How would it look on my mother of the year application if you lost a foot due to frostbite?"

Ashley smiled. She didn't want to let in the least ray of joy, but her mother could always make her laugh. With great effort, Ashley sat up in bed. The room began spinning a little. A wave of nausea swept over her. Quickly, she jumped to her feet and headed for the bathroom in the hallway.

"That's the spirit," her mother said, mistaking Ashley's haste for a changed attitude.

Kneeling next to the toilet, Ashley ejected the remains of her dinner from the night before and quite a bit of Mountain Dew. When finished, she flushed and rinsed her mouth with water and then mouthwash. As she exited the bathroom, she hoped her mother had gone downstairs. She hadn't.

"I didn't realize you were sick. You know, a lot of times when we are feeling down, it's the precursor to getting a cold or the flu or something. Let me make you some tea."

"Mom, come sit with me a minute," Ashley said. "I'm not sick. Come and sit here."

She complied and sat on the edge of the bed. Ashley loved her mother's hazel eyes, shining like two bright beacons in a dark, scary future. In an unusually emotive gesture, Mrs. Featherstone put a gentle arm around her daughter. Ashley felt warm and safe.

"I have to tell you something, and it isn't going to be easy," Ashley said.

"Okay. Try me. You know I'm a pretty strong, resilient woman."

"Mom, I was having sex with Terrell. We loved each other very much, planned to get married someday."

Mrs. Featherstone paused a moment. Then, she offered the most compassionate smile Ashley ever remembered seeing from her. "It's okay. I understand. That makes the pain of losing him even deeper for you."

"That's true, Mom. My soul feels like it's been yanked from my body. When I'm not hurting, I feel dead so far down in my soul. It feels like I can't breathe."

Hugging Ashley again, she stroked the girl's long, blonde hair. "You've experienced a major trauma. Don't expect to get over it in a few days. Lean on me and your family. Think about your faith. You know that God understands us humans better than we suppose. He can and will forgive anything, if we just ask Him."

"I've asked. Believe me, God and I discuss little else these days. What if Terrell's death and all this sorrow came on us because of my sins? We knew it wasn't right to have sex before marriage."

"He's not some petty old codger. God's a loving father. Do you understand that He forgave you the moment you first asked?"

"Yes," Ashley said honestly. "I guess I understand, but it's not that simple. Here's the thing: I'm pregnant."

Her mother's face turned ashen, and her posture changed. Her shoulders slumped forward a bit. No words came out of her mouth. Ashley searched for a hint of the love that was flowing freely from her mother just a few moments earlier. Then, tears began to fall from the eyes of both women.

"I don't know what to do, Mom. Terrell and I went to a women's clinic. I even scheduled an abortion."

"Oh, my goodness," her mother said. "Are you kidding? Without telling me?"

"We couldn't go through with it. Terrell had misgivings. He wanted me to keep the baby, to get married."

"What about school, your future?"

"That's what I told him. Abortion didn't seem like the right idea, but I'm not ready to be a mom. My life is about cheerleading and studying for tests and laughing with Marcella. What am I going to do?"

Mrs. Featherstone offered no easy answers. The two of them just sat together, occasionally hugged, and let more tears fall. The mother and daughter could have stayed there a lot longer, but Mr. Featherstone returned with the donuts. So as not to attract suspicion, both women dried their eyes before heading downstairs.

They all sat around the kitchen island and ate one sugary confection after another. Ashley didn't feel ready to bring her father into the discussion, but that would happen soon enough. The sweetness of the Boston cream donuts melted some of her pain.

28

In the darkness, Detectives Lawson and English carefully made their way down the riverbank. Lawson slipped a couple of times in the mud and snow. A police dive team stood off to the side, apparently packing up their oxygen tanks and other gear. English flashed his badge to the diver who had pulled his wetsuit down to his waist. Toweling off while Lawson caught up, the diver asked "Are you the detectives?"

"Yes, I'm Detective English, and my partner is Lawson. What could you see down there?"

"My name's Scott McCausey, Springfield Sheriff's Dive Team. The river has low visibility on a good day. Tonight, I couldn't see much below the surface. Dispatch got a

report of a body snagged on that large branch out there."
McCausey pointed to a large tree limb stuck on a sandbar
in the middle of the river.

"What time did you guys get here?"

"The call came in just after dusk. We rolled at 6:30
p.m. and got in the water at 7:08. We spotted the body
from the shore and simply swam out to it. Excuse me a
minute." McCausey opened the van door and stripped off
the rest of the wet suit. He quickly donned a sweatshirt
and warm-up pants. He toweled off his hair, turning back
in the direction of the dectectives.

"Was the body fresh?"

"Negative," McCausey said. "She had been in the water
at least a day or two, some bloating and a little decompo-
sition around the face. My partner and I swam her back
over here and drug her up on shore. I took a quick look
around the river bottom near the island, but I couldn't
see anything unusual. With the sandy bottom and low
visibility, I wouldn't swear that there is nothing else down
there, but we couldn't find anything."

"The bridge is about 300 meters upriver," Det. English
said. "Do you think the body could have been dumped
there?"

"Possible," McCausey replied. "It might have come
from anywhere upstream. This time of year, not that
many people hang out down by the river. We got lucky.
A couple of teenage boys spotted the body while fishing
off the riverbank."

Just then, two women from the coroner's office
approached, carrying the remains in a body bag. Det.
English looked in their direction, but decided to wait for
the medical examiner's report for more information about
the body. The coroner's office staff seldom gave substantive
answers on the scene. Lawson didn't bother to try.

Back in their unmarked car, Lawson and English drove to the bridge upstream. They parked on one side of the river and made their way on foot toward the middle of the bridge. As they hugged the left guardrail, a car drove speedily in their direction. Fortunately, the driver saw them walking and swerved to miss them. Near the middle of the span, Det. Lawson used his flashlight as a pointer.

"Look there, possibly some blood."

Both men knelt down and English used his pocket knife to chip off a few red flakes, depositing them in his handkerchief. They followed a trail of blood about eight feet farther. Then the trail of dried blood stopped.

"Do you see the stain on top of the railing?" Lawson asked.

"Yep, we need a csi over here to dust for prints and collect a proper sample," English replied.

English called back to the station house to request the csi meet them. Meanwhile, Lawson walked the rest of the way across the bridge. A few feet past where the body may have gone over the railing, he saw a piece of torn fabric hooked on a metal screw protruding from the railing structure. He collected the sample by prying it loose with his pen and saving it in a small envelope from his back pocket.

Although he detected nothing else on the bridge itself, he walked the rest of the way across. His diligence paid off when he got to the other side.

"English, there appears to be a car run off the road here. Can you see it from where you are standing?"

"Negative," Det. English shouted. "When the csi shows up, I will send her over there as well."

Det. Lawson could barely make out the outline of the car from his perch next to the roadway. He followed a crude staircase made of rocks and cuts in the clay, probably created by fishermen wanting to get access to the river. Once down by the river, he pushed through underbrush to the abandoned vehicle. Despite a light covering of frost on the windows, he could tell no one occupied the front seats.

Walking around the hood of the car, he recorded the license plate number and called it in to dispatch. To his surprise, he heard faint whimpering coming from inside the vehicle. Det. Lawson rushed to get a better look in the backseat. To his horror, he spied a car seat. A dazed-looking infant stared blankly forward. Grabbing a rock, he beat on the rear driver's side window until it broke into pebbles. Reaching down, he unlocked the door. Using all his grandpa skills, he quickly unfastened the car seat restraints and retrieved the shivering baby.

"Call dispatch, we need an ambulance right away," Det. Lawson yelled up to English.

While his partner requested a medical assist, Lawson placed the baby next to his body inside his topcoat. The infant felt cool to the touch, but not cold. Within just a few minutes of Lawson climbing up to the bridge, an ambulance pulled in, sirens blaring. Paramedics took over and rushed the child to the hospital.

"The vehicle is registered to Judith Kramer." Detective Lawson relayed the information to his partner. "Dispatch informs that Kramer's mother filed a Missing Person report yesterday morning. It looks like the baby could have been in the car for 36 to 48 hours."

"Whoever ditched the vehicle is either one heartless son of a gun or just didn't notice the baby in the backseat," Detective English added.

"Let's swing by the home of the victim's mother and see what she knows," Det. Lawson suggested. "We can offer to transport her to the hospital so she can check on the child."

After a fifteen-minute ride to the Fenwick subdivision, the detectives arrived at a humble three-bedroom ranch. Peeling teal paint around the front door indicated the house could use a bit of upkeep.

Flashing his badge and introducing himself, Detective Lawson asked, "Did you file a Missing Person report on Judith Kramer?"

"Yes, is something wrong?" A diminutive woman with graying hair and a meek voice invited the men inside. Although wearing a bathrobe, she didn't look sleepy or even disheveled.

"Does your daughter drive a red Chevrolet Impala?" Det. English asked.

"Yes. Did you find her car? Is Judith alright?" The woman's voice quivered and trailed off.

"We believe we have recovered your daughter's car near the river," Det. Lawson said. "A drowning victim also was recovered nearby. We don't know for sure if it's your daughter. The body was in the river for a while."

"Oh Jesus. Hold me, Lord. What about her baby? Was the baby found in the river too?"

"No, ma'am," Det. Lawson said. "I found the baby alive in his car seat. He's been taken to Springfield Children's for treatment."

"Judith would never willingly leave her baby in the car. What happened? How did she get in the river?"

"We don't know just yet. Can you think of anyone that might wish to harm Judith?"

"No. While I wouldn't call her the most likeable person in the world, I can't see anyone wanting to hurt her."

Det. English leaned in toward the couch where Judith's mother sat. "Is your grandson's father living? Can you give us an address for him?"

"Fred is alive, last we heard. No one has any idea where he's at—hiding out a thousand miles from here probably. Not long after Judith got pregnant, Fred took off. He's technically still married to Judith. Truthfully, he is an addict and has the sense of a 13-year-old. The last thing he wanted was a baby and responsibilities. Judith thought about getting an abortion—even went to that women's clinic in town. She couldn't go through with it and canceled at the last minute. I felt so glad she kept her baby. He's been a blessing to all of us, the only light in our lives some days."

"As the next of kin, are you able to care for the boy in case he's released from the hospital right away?"

"Oh, my goodness yes. I wouldn't want him to go anywhere else. We have all his stuff and his little bed here."

"My partner and I will take you over to the hospital if you like," Det. English said. "We will wait while you get ready."

"It will only take a few minutes," she said.

29

The doorbell interrupted Madison's cleaning ritual. Every morning, she cleaned up the kitchen after breakfast while the kids played in the dining room. Stopping to answer the door amounted to a minor irritation.

"Mrs. Matthews, you remember us, Detectives Lawson and my partner, English?"

"Of course, please come in."

"We were in the neighborhood and wondered if we could ask a couple of follow-up questions."

"Detective Lawson, sure, but Zane isn't here right now. I have small children, so try to be careful what you say while they play nearby."

"No problem."

The two men followed her into the kitchen and sat at the island where she directed them. Madison peeked in on the children and smiled, seeing Shelby serving imaginary tea to Braden.

"What can I do for you gentlemen?"

"Another victim has turned up." Det. English said. "Have you ever met a lady named Judith Kramer?"

"No, her name doesn't ring a bell," Madison said. "Should I know her?"

"We understand she considered having an abortion through the clinic where you work," Det. English said.

"Actually, I'm no longer with Planned Parenthood. I'm a full-time, stay-at-home mom now. Do you know about how long ago she might have visited the clinic?"

"Probably about two years ago," Det. Lawson said.

"That would explain it," Madison said. "I only worked there for about 11 months. I quit last week. She would have been before my time. It's disturbing to hear of another victim though. Including Terrell, that makes four? And they all have some connection to the clinic?"

"Yes. All of them had some business with the clinic. Each of the women and Terrell's girlfriend considered abortion, but decided against it. Terrell's situation, of course, is a little different. Do you know why anyone would want to kill people associated with the clinic? Particularly people who cancelled their procedures?"

"Well, a whole cast of characters protest outside the clinic two days a week," Madison said. "They may not know for sure whether or not a client had a procedure or cancelled. If someone just took down license numbers and tracked down the patients, I suppose that's one plausible explanation."

"Do you mind me asking why you stopped working at the clinic?" Lawson asked, raising his sizable eyebrows.

"Not at all," Madison said. "I'm pregnant. This will be my third, and I plan to become a stay-at-home mom."

"Oh," Lawson said while staring into his notepad.

"I have to ask this," Det. English said. "Is there anyone at the clinic or maybe a spouse of one of the clinic workers who you suspect may be capable of these crimes?"

Madison rubbed her right temple. "Honestly, I don't think so. There are so few of us really. Madge runs the clinic. She is single and totally focused on the organization's success. I doubt she would do anything to jeopardize the reputation of the Women's Clinic. Vanessa serves as receptionist, scheduler, insurance guru, etc. She just isn't the angry type. I don't know her husband, but from her stories—he sounds pretty normal. Vanessa's husband coaches little league soccer. Dr. Heller, who performs the abortions, is my gynecologist. He's got to be in his sixties at least. He definitely doesn't like cancellations, but he's got to be sixty-five at least. I have trouble picturing him running down athletic women on the jogging path, let alone having the strength to strangle them. Besides, he's part-time. That leaves only his nurse, Natasha. She also works for the clinic just one day a week. Doesn't seem likely for the same reasons I'd rule out Dr. Heller. She wouldn't have sufficient strength or motivation."

"Okay," English said. "If you think of anything else that might help, give us a call."

Lawson and English departed, but Madison didn't stop thinking about the rising body count or the possible identity of the Springfield Strangler.

30

The Thanksgiving break came at just the right time for Ashley. Although back at school only two weeks, she felt emotionally exhausted trying to keep her secret, catch up on school work, fight off morning sickness, and decide what to do about her pregnancy.

On the one hand, having the procedure felt like a betrayal of Terrell's memory and legacy. If she terminated her pregnancy, a piece of him would be gone. If she had the baby, a part of Terrell could live on. Perhaps she might meet another guy who could be a good husband to her and a loving father to her son or daughter. Although not in the picture, she knew Terrell would vote to have the baby.

Conversely, Ashley's mother and father lobbied her

every few days to seriously consider an abortion. As a high school senior, she could forget the past and start over at the college of her choice. Her grades and SAT scores opened several doors from nearby Ohio State to schools as far away as UCLA. Although her parents hadn't said as much, a decision to have her baby would probably mean staying close to home. With a more local school, her mother could help care for the child while Ashley attended classes and worked a part-time job.

The doorbell broke her chain of thought. It indicated the first guests arriving for their family Thanksgiving dinner. Her older brother and his fiancée showed up first. She looked forward to being with Trevor and Sally. They were always full of stories and humorous asides about working for large corporations, living in the city, or young-adult life. Having met at Penn State in an accounting class, they joked about being the most boring couple in their college neighborhood.

Within thirty minutes, Ashley's maternal grandparents joined the party, bringing grandmother's famous pineapple upside-down cake. Grandpa told his first joke about flatulence before the hors d'oerves made their first pass around the room.

Once everyone gathered around the table, Ashley kept her eyes open during the prayer. She wanted to take it all in. Her father looked so sweet as he bowed his head and said grace. Just having everyone together like this made her happy and sad at the same time. Would she spoil the innocence of their family gatherings once the rest of the relatives learned of her pregnancy? She brushed away a tear or two before anyone noticed.

As soon as her father said "amen," the food passed quickly around the table. Crescent rolls—not burned this year—remained Ashley's favorite. She took two and a hefty slice of butter. Not worried about her weight at the moment, generous portions of turkey and dressing landed heavily next to her mashed potatoes and gravy. Finally, corn pudding found its special place in the middle of her plate. Nothing screamed Thanksgiving like Mom's corn pudding.

Forks clinked in a rhythmic melody on the Spode plates. Ashley smiled and even laughed a bit at the light conversation. Finally, everyone slowed down in their eating and things got quiet for a moment.

"I guess this is a good time to tell you that Sally and I have a couple of announcements," Trevor said.

"Wait a minute," Grandpa jumped into the conversation. "You announced your engagement on Memorial Day and told us to expect a spring wedding. Another announcement already?"

"Grandpa, you are correct on both counts," Trevor said. "Now, we want to announce the birth of our first child."

"Really," Ashley said. "I didn't even know Sally was pregnant."

"She isn't. We are adopting a brother and sister from Albania. The mother delivered twins last night. Sally and I plan to fly out tomorrow to pick them up and bring them home."

All sorts of loud congratulations and comments ensued from everyone except Ashley. Her brain nearly exploded thinking about this news. Why hadn't she thought about putting her child up for adoption? Perhaps Trevor and Sally would like to adopt her baby as well. Wait a minute, what was she saying? That's jumping ahead a bit. They didn't even know she had a bun in the oven.

"There is a related announcement," Sally said. "Since we decided not to live together before marriage, we needed to move up our wedding date."

"We actually got married yesterday at city hall," Trevor said. "Show them your ring, honey."

Both Trevor and Sally stuck out their hands and twirled their ring fingers. Everyone started talking at the same time. The longtime Mrs. Featherstone rushed from her seat to embrace the new Mrs. Featherstone.

"There is still going to be a party," Sally said. "My parents are off the hook for a big wedding, but they agreed to throw us a big reception at the venue of our choice around the holidays."

"So, you all are still on the hook for gifts," Trevor said while winking.

After the excitement died down, the men headed off to the den to begin a lengthy game of Risk. Sally, Ashley, and her mother cleaned up the kitchen while Grandma regaled them with tales of her time in Ireland before her stroke.

"Seriously, it turned out to be the best vacation ever," Grandma said. "It's like I can remember every detail of that summer. I'm so glad we did it while we were still healthy enough to do all the hiking and dancing."

"Sally, how did you and Trevor decide to adopt?" Ashley asked. "And why now?"

"Good question," Ashley's mom said, staring over at her daughter.

"Well, that's a fair question," Sally said. "Not long after we started dating, I told Trevor that I would not be able to have my own biological children. In my freshman year of college, severe pain drove me to the doctor. Long story short, I had several cysts on my ovaries. The doctors eventually removed them, and now I can't get pregnant."

"I'm so sorry, dear," Ashley's mother said, patting Sally on the shoulder.

"The news devastated me," Sally said. "After sinking into

depression and dropping out for a semester, I returned to school and ended up in class with Trevor. We fell in love and you know the rest of that part of the story. Well, we both want kids. You know how Trevor is about solving problems and taking life head on? He insisted we attend an adoption workshop that we heard about through our church. Next thing you know, we decided to fill out all the paperwork about six months ago. The average wait time is two to three years. Some couples never get called by the agency. It seemed rather abstract at the time. Making the connection between filling out papers and actually holding a baby—I couldn't really picture it. We imagined ourselves firmly established in jobs and decorating our first home. Surprise! We get a call yesterday. A young woman in Albania was about to give birth to twins, and the couples ahead of us on the agency's list all said no to twins."

"That's an amazing story," Ashley said.

"Trevor and I have lots of love to share," Sally said. "Getting two at once and so early in our lives together seems like a big challenge, but we have peace about it. We know God worked this out for us and for these kids."

"Do you ever wonder how a mother can give up her children?" Ashley asked before really thinking through how the question sounded.

"Ashley!" Her mother interjected, shooting her a serious look.

"It's okay, Mrs. F. I know it seems hard to imagine, but the adoption training explained so much. We all find ourselves in difficult circumstances from time to time. If a young woman becomes pregnant and doesn't want an abortion, adoption is a great option. That's a slogan they use. The child gets a loving home. The mother doesn't have to bring a child into less-than-ideal circumstances or even change her life plans. It costs a few months and there is a toll on the body, but it's such a gift to give a couple who really want children. A beautiful gift. Trevor and I are so thankful."

31

Two days later, Dr. and Mrs. Heller, Cynthia, and Jacob stood on the first tee at Ducktail Country Club. Dr. Heller's first shot exploded off his driver and landed 250 yards down the fairway

"Nice drive, Daddy," Cynthia said.

Going next, Cynthia also hit a respectable drive. Jacob sent his two-iron shot into the trees to the right, slicing it almost comically. Marie hit a 5-iron, plunking the ball about 130 yards straight ahead into the fairway. They went their separate ways to find their balls and hit toward the hole.

Reconvening on the green, Cynthia and Dr. Heller missed medium-length birdie putts. Marie two-putted for a bogie. Jacob found himself in the sand trap, sitting six. He eventually carded a nine. After Cynthia and her father made their pars, they all had to wait at the second tee for the group ahead of them.

"Tell us about your job with Social Security," Dr. Heller said. "Mrs. Heller and I would like to know more about you."

"Well, I work in an office that adjudicates disputes between beneficiaries and the Agency. Usually the disagreement is about how much they were paid or should be paid," Jacob explained. "Sometimes, people appeal a decision to deny disability benefits."

"Are you a lawyer?" Marie asked.

"I graduated from University of Chicago Law School, but my job doesn't require admission to the bar. It's an administrative position. The Administrative Law Judges tell us how they want to rule. Assistants like myself write up rationales to support their decisions."

"How long have you lived in the Chicago area?" Marie asked.

"All my life," Jacob said. "My grandparents moved to Oak Park from Austria in the 1920s. They founded a jewelry store, which my parents eventually sold and bought an electronics store. The family business paid my way through undergrad and gave me a summer job each year. I owe my family a lot of gratitude and respect."

"Glad to hear you give them some credit, unlike Cynthia with her old dad," Dr. Heller said.

"Oh, Daddy!" Cynthia complained.

"Actually, your daughter speaks quite glowingly about you, sir. She says you've stuck by her through good times and bad."

"See Daddy. I don't bad-mouth you to others."

"You just argue with me face to face," Dr. Heller replied.

"Look honey, the foursome ahead of us moved on," Marie said, hoping to change the subject.

Everyone teed off and went their separate ways up the course. At the third tee, it turned into another waiting game with the group ahead, including a couple of novice golfers.

"I hate waiting at every tee," Dr. Heller said.

"It's okay, we can enjoy the time getting to know Jacob," Marie said.

"The main things in my life right now are church and Cynthia," Jacob said. "We are very involved in our fellowship, host a home group, and put in one Saturday morning a month to feed the homeless. Our pastors are great guys. Hope you two can join us for a service when you visit Cynthia."

"That would be lovely," Marie said.

"Oh yes, lovely," Dr. Heller muttered, rolling his eyes.

"Sir, you don't have to worry about what anyone thinks of you being an abortionist," Jacob said.

Cynthia gritted her teeth at the word *abortionist*.

"Don't worry about it," Dr. Heller said. "I don't have a moment's guilt about the judgment of hypocritical church people. The same ones that go to church around here visit the clinic for procedures so the husband won't figure out the baby isn't his. No shame on my part."

"My former pastor used to say, don't let hypocrites at church get you down," Cynthia said. "One more won't matter."

Marie shot Cynthia a look.

"Just the same, we'd love to have you meet our church friends," Jacob said.

Fortunately, the group ahead of Dr. Heller quit after the fourth hole, greatly speeding up the pace of play.

32

Pulling up in the driveway, Madison had no idea what awaited her in the house. *Why aren't Zane and the kids home yet? Why is he always later than expected whenever the kids are involved? How could I not love a man who delights himself in his children?*

She did the math in her head. *Let's see, he was supposed to pick them up at 4:30 at Mom's house, almost an hour ago.* This gave Madison time for extra Christmas shopping without Shelby asking endless questions or begging for everything in the toy section.

Flipping the switch in the living room produced no improvement to the oppressive darkness. *How could the bulb in that lamp be out again?* Setting her packages down on the sofa, she headed for the kitchen. This time, the lights above the island responded and lit up the counter area. Madison quickly spotted the note from Zane. "No need to make dinner. Your mom is feeding us. We will bring home leftovers." Welcome news. Madison pulled off her shoes and set them to the side.

Turning around, she froze in horror.

"What are you doing in my house?"

Dr. Heller stood only three feet away. The look on his face horrified Madison. Like the time in the procedure room at the clinic, he appeared cold, detached. She could smell garlic on his breath.

"My husband will be home any minute. You better get out of here. I *will* call the police."

"No, you won't," Dr. Heller said. "Your phone is in your purse in the other room."

Now growing more terrified, Madison rushed to the counter with the knife drawer. Dr. Heller followed hot on her heels. She felt a pin prick on the back of her arm. Reaching in the drawer, she desperately looked down, trying to identify the right knife to defend herself from her attacker. Before she could select one, Dr. Heller backed away.

"Where are you going?" she asked. Her voice sounded like it was in slow motion. That was the last thing she remembered.

******

When Zane arrived home, he wasn't surprised that Madison hadn't made it yet. She probably got held up at the mall. He pulled into his usual spot in the garage. After helping Shelby out of her car seat, he set his daughter down and walked to the door which leads from the garage to the house. After unlocking it, he sent Shelby inside by herself.

Zane retrieved Braden and the meal Madison's mom had thoughtfully packed. Inside, Zane noticed that Shelby had dropped her coat on the stairs and headed straight for the family room. The light in the living room didn't work, so he climbed the stairs in the dark. Placing Braden in his crib without waking him, Zane turned on the baby monitor and headed back downstairs.

After turning on the lights in the kitchen, he saw Shelby sitting in front of the television in the family room watching an animated show.

"Do you need to go to the bathroom, Shelby?" he asked.

"I don't think so, Daddy," she replied.

Zane retrieved Madison's food from the living room and brought it into the kitchen. *Maybe Madison will hurry home if she knows her mother's meatloaf is waiting.* Deciding to give her a call, he pulled out his phone, but saw he had a message from Det. English. He decided to return his call first.

"Detective English, this is Zane Matthews. Did you call me?"

"Yes, Mr. Matthews. We want to alert you and your wife. Some disturbing DNA evidence came to our attention from one of the recent murders. I can't tell you more at this moment, but we plan to make an arrest in the morning. It's important that the two of you be vigilant this evening. We don't have specific reason to believe you are in immediate danger, but as a precaution, I've requested that a patrol car swing past your house. Again, don't be alarmed. Just stay in tonight and hopefully, we will have some good news for you tomorrow morning."

"Okay," Zane said.

The call unsettled him a little. Feeling some urgency to contact Madison, he dialed her number from his contacts and waited for the phone to ring. In seconds, her phone rang in the kitchen drawer, just a few feet from where Zane stood. He raced to the counter and yanked open the knife drawer. The sight and sound of her phone ringing sent shivers up his spine. She never went anywhere without her phone, yet here it sat ringing in, of all places, the knife drawer. *Why would she leave it there?* The bigger question: where is Madison?

33

The road and everything around it seemed shrouded in thick fog. Billows of dark shadows and white fog prevented Madison from finding her way through the dense cloak of night. *There is something I must do, but what is it?* she thought. Shelby must be in trouble…or Braden. The children are in danger somehow. Madison must raise her hand to her head. If she could just rub her throbbing temple, the headache might disappear and clear thinking replace this fog. Her hand wouldn't move.

"You're waking up a little, I see."

The voice sounded familiar. A kind voice from the past. Whose is it? She knew, but the name wouldn't come to her at first.

"Wakey, wakey," Dr. Heller said. "I want you to be wide awake for your procedure."

Reality came flooding in like a tidal wave. Madison realized she should be trying to run away. First, she must get her hands free. *What is going on?*

"Where am I?" Madison asked.

"Look around. Don't you find this place familiar?" Dr. Heller said. "It's where you first discovered this other side of me. Like most people, I'm made of shadows and light. For years, you saw only the light. No picture is complete without understanding the importance of shadow."

Madison tried to focus her mind, but she couldn't even control her eyes. The acoustic tiles on the ceiling meant she must be restrained on a table at the Planned Parenthood clinic. Looking to the left, she saw the ultrasound reader, the same one she used during Dee's abortion. Panic began to build. Restraints held her wrists to the gurney. Fighting with every ounce of strength yielded no result against the heavy, leather restraints.

Looking down, she saw that her pants were missing. Dr. Heller finished taping her feet into the stirrups. Her first instinct took over, and she violently fought against her restraints. For sixty, then ninety seconds, she battled with all her will to no avail. She remained at the mercy of this demented excuse for a doctor.

"Very good," he said. "You recognize where you are now. It's time for your procedure. I've decided two children are enough for you."

The old man laughed maniacally. He turned on the ultrasound and squirted jelly on Madison's abdomen.

"You are a madman!" Madison screamed. "Why are you doing this?

"Just relax," Dr. Heller said. "Everyone gets cold feet right before their abortion. You may even want to cancel,

but that won't be an option. You aren't going to be one
of those women who try to cancel and run off at the last
minute? How rude! Here I am, donating my time this
evening so you can get rid of the little problem you have
growing inside. The least you can do is lie back and take
it like a woman." His laughter indicated the depths of
his debauchery.

Placing the wand on her midsection, an image of a
small fetus projected onto the screen.

"No, not my baby!" Madison sobbed thinking of what
might come next.

"You see, Mrs. Matthews, you are a member of the
ignorant masses. I didn't think you were when I met you
years ago. Lately, I've changed my mind. Even though
you don't live in a ghetto, your trash just like the others."

Composing herself, Madison looked her tormenter
in the eye. "I've changed my mind about you, too, Dr.
Heller. You've gone mad, just a crazy old fool. The police
are coming any minute. You have to know my husband
will stop at nothing until he finds me. When he does, you
are going to be extremely sorry."

"Mr. Matthews won't be coming," Dr. Heller said. "He's
indisposed. Women like you can't expect a man to bail
you out. You just don't understand life ... what's good for
you. That little wiggler inside is likely to grow up just as
messed up as you. It's a boy, by the way. Your son will be in
a plastic medical waste tub a few short minutes from now."

Madison screamed out in terror. Then, she reached
back in her past to a place she hadn't been in a long time.
"Dear Jesus, help me. I'm walking through the valley of
the shadow of death. Save me."

"Oh, isn't that rich," Dr. Heller said. "Jesus doesn't care
about the likes of you and me, Mrs. Matthews. There's
no hope for you in God. You don't have a prayer. Do you

think Jesus can forgive all those little lives you had a hand in killing? I did the procedures, but you led the women to the slaughterhouse. Like a pied piper, you are just as guilty as I am. We will rot in hell together... if you think there is such a thing. I don't."

Madison didn't reply. Tears poured from her eyes. What if she *had* passed a point of no return? Would she die now apart from God? She prayed silently for forgiveness, for a way out.

"You superstitious fool. What you don't understand is that God can't help you now," Dr. Heller said. "He's left me in charge in this town. Mighty fine job I've done, too. I delivered all the future doctors, senators, even the truck drivers. I started them on their way like roses growing in Marie's garden. I've also weeded out the bad seeds. That's the problem with our world – too many weeds. Now, we are going to send just one more little wiggler into oblivion. Then, I plan to retire for good. Marie and I might take a cruise around the world. No more ungrateful women like you. I'm done with all of you."

"Look, I beg you," Madison pleaded, "I will give you anything: money, whatever you want. Let me buy your cruise with your wife."

"You are really missing my point, young lady. My goal has never been riches. All I want is to make a meaningful contribution. Your ilk wants to cloud the picture, steal the glory for what is rightfully mine. Even my own daughter doesn't appreciate my gift to the world. Tonight, you will have a front row seat for abortion number 1,500. Nice round number to call it a career, I think."

For a moment, Dr. Heller turned his back to retrieve the surgical instruments. Without a nurse to help him, he just dumped the contents of the drawer out on a metal tray. It landed with a loud, clanking sound, startling Madison.

She prayed once more, trying to think of anything to delay Dr. Heller. Surely, Zane and the police must be searching. Pulling with all of her might, her right hand came free. Nothing was within reach and Heller already began turning around.

"Dr. Heller, do want this to be your legacy? After all you believe that you've done for our town, the only thing people will remember is how you went nuts at the end and killed a patient?"

"They will say nothing of the kind, Mrs. Matthews. You see, I want you to live and to testify to my final contribution here tonight. I'll let everyone know my plan to rid the town of undesirables and show how successful I've been."

As he spoke, Heller rolled the cart with the metal tray of instruments near to the operating table. As he raised the sheet to access Madison's lower body, she saw a razor-thin window of opportunity. The sheet blocked his view of the instrument tray. Madison carefully, quietly slipped a scalpel off the tray.

"This won't take long," Dr. Heller said as he turned on the suction device.

Madison knew the element of surprise would be her only advantage. Just as Dr. Heller leaned between her legs and touched her for the first time, she lunged as fast and hard as she could. The scalpel made contact, but Madison couldn't tell if she'd actually cut him at first. He recoiled and stood up. In doing so, she ripped the scalpel along Dr. Heller's neck.

In the process, Madison dropped the scalpel on the sheet near her stomach. She unbuckled the restraint on her left hand. Ripping the sheet away, she got her first good look at Dr. Heller after she cut him. Blood spurted and oozed out of a cut on his neck. She picked up the scalpel and began cutting the tape binding her right foot and leg.

Dr. Heller gathered himself from the floor and rushed at Madison. She grabbed the only thing near her. The metal tray holding the instruments proved a sturdy shield. She raised it between herself and Dr. Heller. His strength significant, Madison fought like a champion to see her children and husband again.

The doctor wrestled the tray from Madison and swung it wildly in her direction. The tray made a sickening crunching sound as it hit her head. With her left arm, she partially blocked a second blow of the tray as she again picked up the scalpel. The sharp tool sliced into her attacker's wrist, bringing another issue of blood, forcing its way from his body. Suddenly, Dr. Heller stopped in his tracks. He stared at his arm. Blood trickled down to the floor, and he stared at it.

"You hurt me." His words accompanied a look of disbelief. As horrifically as her ordeal began in the operating room, it ended with little fanfare. Dr. Heller retreated to the side table, picked up a roll of white tape, and exited the room, looking baffled.

Madison quickly cut her other leg and foot free from the stirrups. She rushed to the door of the operating room and slammed it shut in case the doctor tried to return. As she locked the door, she pushed the ultrasound machine over to the door and braced herself against it.

In a few minutes, she heard a car start in the parking lot and drive off. Could it be that Dr. Heller just drove away? Unsure, she stayed in the operating room for several minutes. Finally, Madison carefully moved the heavy machine away, and, with the scalpel in hand, crept down the hall to the front of the clinic. She picked up the phone on Vanessa's reception desk. A digital clock glowed green in her field of vision.

"This is 9-1-1, what is your emergency."

"I've been attacked. Please send police to the Springfield Women's Clinic on Clifford Street. Hurry!"

34

Two hours later, Marie Heller heard loud knocking at her front door. She made her way downstairs. "Just a minute; I'm coming," she said.

Opening the door, Detectives Lawson and English flashed their badges. Uniformed officers followed them into the foyer.

"Ma'am, where's Dr. Heller?" Detective Lawson said. "We need to speak with him immediately."

"He's upstairs," Marie said. "He went to bed over an hour ago. I will tell him you're here."

"That won't be necessary," English said as he and the others pushed by her and rapidly climbed the stairs.

Seeing only one closed door, the officers turned the

knob and rushed in with their guns drawn.

"Dr. Heller, this is Detective Lawson, Springfield Police Department."

At first, there seemed no sign of Dr. Heller. The bed empty, one of the officers turned on the light. On the wall, a large chunk of plaster had been beaten away. Flecks of blood dotted the wall, the carpet, and the footboard of the bed. As Lawson approached the far side of the king bed, he found the doctor crumpled to the floor. His lifeless body clutched a hammer. Lawson reached down for a pulse but didn't find one. Heller's body felt cold to the touch. He was gone.

35

Months later, Sarah Warren opened the door and welcomed Ashley Featherstone inside. After hanging up Ashley's coat, the two walked to the living room. A delicate teapot and cups sat on a silver tray atop the coffee table. A platter of blueberry scones beckoned as well.

Madison stood up from the couch and, bending forward, awkwardly embraced Ashley. The two women held that position for several seconds.

"Glad to see you, Ashley," Sarah said.

Madison smiled as the other two women sat down. Both Ashley and Madison looked a bit physically uncomfortable. Their sizable baby bumps indicated impending deliveries. Sarah poured each woman a cup of green tea and placed a scone on the matching plates.

"Thank you," Ashley said. "The scones look amazing. Thank you. I feel so loved and welcomed every week."

"You certainly are welcome," Sarah said. "I appreciate you both so much. These last months have been such a blessing. Even though this is our last official meeting, I hope each of you will stop by anytime in the future. I can always take a break from my Accounting work and put on a kettle of tea."

With that, the ladies opened their books and began studying the last lesson: Godliness with Contentment. Madison polished off her scone quickly, while Ashley timidly nibbled one small bite at a time. When the meat of the Bible lesson concluded, the conversation turned to Ashley and her big decision.

"Now's the part of the meeting when we each talk about how things are going," Madison said. "I have a follow-up with my doctor later this week. Pray that all goes well. If she thinks I'm too far along, she may want to induce labor. This is the perfect last lesson for me. It's been an adjustment staying home after getting a taste of the working life. Don't get me wrong, I love caring for the kids and having a healthy dinner ready for Zane. Part of me is still a little restless."

"That's understandable," Sarah said. "It's an adjustment. You just have to look at it for what it is…a season of your life. We all feel many emotions in every phase of life. Finding that sweet spot with God is difficult part: cherishing each day and not looking too far ahead. How about you, Ashley? Did you make a final decision about your adoption plans?"

"Yes. Before I tell you the particulars, there is some other exciting news I'd like to share. You know how hard it's been since Terrell's been gone. My Dad had a great idea. We are going to have a golf tournament in honor of Terrell. The proceeds will go to the Pro-life Action League of Clark County."

"Wow. What a great idea," Sarah said. "You can keep his memory alive and raise money for a cause that represents his memory."

"Absolutely. He wanted me to have the baby. Rather than have some morbid remembrance ceremony, this can be a more positive event that shares his heart for the unborn."

"That's such a beautiful idea," Madison said. "Now quit torturing us. What did you decide about who's adopting your baby?"

First, let me say how much your support has meant to me through these many weeks. The decision to carry the child to term took a lot of thinking, praying, and above all, convincing my parents. For so long, I thought the only choice was to abort or not. Hearing about my brother and his wife's journey with adoption opened me up to other possibilities. He and his wife offered to adopt my son too. Although it is tempting to take him up on it, I think the child would choose a fresh start – without complications. So would I. My plan is to go to college in the fall."

"Praise God," Sarah said. "I believe you made a wise decision."

"Me too," Madison affirmed.

"Madison, I love that you helped me see the joy of the pregnancy phase," Ashley said. "Meeting here with you and Sarah once a week got my eyes off the birth and onto the joy of living each day one at a time. My family and I have spent hours going over the possibilities of having my brother and his wife either temporarily or permanently raise my child. At first, I thought it would be awkward being in my child's life, but not acting as his mother. That could create a level of complexity for all of us, but particularly for the child. What age is a good one to learn that your aunt is really your mother?"

"Yes," Sarah said reassuringly. "You've had a lot to think about."

"Since God opened my eyes about His love for this baby, I've tried to think what would the baby prefer? What if the baby really did have the right to choose which life he wanted to live? Since he's obviously not old enough to make that decision, God left me to choose on his behalf. I decided to give him up to a Christian adoption agency. My brother and his wife are wonderful people, but they are newlyweds. They thought they would adopt one child a couple of years into their marriage. Instead, they moved up their wedding date and started their marriage with twins. Adding a third child months later would be a lot to ask. If it were my decision as a baby, I think I would prefer to have my own parents without the complications that come with an aunt who's also my mother."

"It sounds like you've completely thought and prayed this through," Madison said. "I'm sure God is honored by your decision. You are doing what you think best for your child and for your future too."

"I plan to finish up high school on-line and begin classes at UCLA in the fall," Ashley continued. "Thanks to God and both of you, my life is changed forever. What could have been the end of me has become a happy time of getting to know God and myself. Whatever the West Coast holds for me, I know Jesus will be there with me."

"I'm so happy for you," Sarah said. "What about you, Madison? After the baby, do you have any plans?"

"These last six months have brought so much change," Madison said. "Following the ordeal with Dr. Heller, I'm just about now starting to feel normal again around the house. That poor man must have had a complete mental breakdown. I'm looking forward to just being a mom for a couple of years. Zane and I love being back in church again. Shelby is so happy with all the children's activities on Sunday mornings."

"That's great," Sarah said. "It sounds like we've all made some big decisions in the past few months."

"I know Ashley and I have made big decisions, but what changes have you been deciding on?"

"Well, it seemed too early in the game to tell you before. Mr. Hastings from my church, you that widower guy who asked me out a month ago?"

"Yes," Madison said smiling from ear to ear.

"He asked me to marry him and I accepted his proposal." Sarah reached out her hand to reveal a beautiful diamond engagement ring."

"That's so exciting," Ashley said, struggling to get up off of her seat.

Madison helped Ashley stand and the three women hugged it out for a few moments.

"Before we say a temporary goodbye, I have a present for each of you." Sarah Warren walked to her side boy and retrieved two books covered in brown wrapping and tied with pink twine. Both women eagerly opened their gift.

"Oh, thank you! A journal!" Madison said, elated. "I've been meaning to get one."

"I have very special instructions," Sarah added. "Instead of just writing out your thoughts, share your heart with God. Write your prayers, your hopes and even your complaints. Let God know your hopes, your praises, your dreams, and your requests. Trust Him with your innermost thoughts. Then, remember to write down the answers in the margin. I've been doing this for years. He reminds me sometimes of prayers He answers that I'd forgotten about asking."

After promising Sarah that they would indeed use their journals, Madison said a hopeful closing prayer. The three women exchanged final hugs, and Sarah walked the women out to their cars. She stood waving on the sidewalk as Ashley and Madison each drove away. Sarah looked up to her Father in heaven and just smiled. This felt like the abundant life she'd prayed for when her first husband passed away. Godliness with contentment? *Yes, it's a thing.*

Epilog

If you are facing a difficult choice about your pregnancy, help is available. In addition to the many pro-life state and local crisis pregnancy centers, National Right to Life wants to help at www.nrlc.org.

Other Books by David L. Winters

Fiction

Driver Confessional

Stock Car Inferno

Five Christmas Plays (With Joy Inside)

Non-Fiction

Exercise Your Faith

Taking God to Work (The Keys to Ultimate Success)
with Steve Reynolds

The Accidental Missionary (A Gringo's Love Affair with
Peru) with David Bredeman

Sabbatical of the Mind (The Journey from Anxiety to
Faith)

Compilations

All God's Creatures Daily Devotional 2019, 2020,
2021—Published by Guideposts

CPSIA information can be obtained
at www.ICGtesting.com
Printed in the USA
FSHW010731071120
75528FS

9 781733 924061